Journey to Mount Tamalpais, Second Edition, Litmus Press, 2021

Shifting the Silence, Nightboat Books, 2020

Time, Nightboat Books, 2019

Surge, Nightboat Books, 2018

Night, Nightboat Books, 2016

Life is a Weaving, Galerie Lelong, 2016

Premonition, Kelsey Street Press, 2014

Sea & Fog, Nightboat Books, 2012

Master of the Eclipse, Interlink Books, 2009

In the Heart of the Heart of Another Country, City Lights Books, 2005

Seasons, The Post-Apollo Press, 2005

In/somnia, The Post-Apollo Press, 2002

There, The Post-Apollo Press, 1997

Of Cities & Women (Letters to Fawwaz), The Post-Apollo Press, 1993

Paris, When It's Naked, The Post-Apollo Press, 1993

The Spring Flowers Own & The Manifestations of the Voyage,
        The Post-Apollo Press, 1990

The Arab Apocalypse, The Post-Apollo Press, 1989

Journey to Mount Tamalpais, The Post-Apollo Press, 1986

The Indian Never Had a Horse & Other Poems, The Post-Apollo Press, 1985

Sitt Marie-Rose, The Post-Apollo Press, 1982

From A to Z, The Post-Apollo Press, 1982

Five Senses for One Death, The Smith, New York 1971

Moonshots, Beirut 1966

PARIS, WHEN IT'S NAKED

PARIS, WHEN IT'S NAKED

Etel Adnan

THE POST-APOLLO PRESS / LITMUS PRESS

Paris, When It's Naked © Etel Adnan, 1993
Fourth Printing, 2022

ISBN: 978-0-942996-20-3

Cover photograph by Simone Fattal
Book design by Simone Fattal

Composed by Michael Sykes at Archetype West,
Point Reyes, California.

The Post-Apollo Press was founded by Simone Fattal in 1982. It is now
managed by Litmus Press and distributed by Small Press Distribution in
Berkeley, CA. *Paris, When It's Naked* is a Post-Apollo Press reprint
published by Litmus Press.

Litmus Press publications are made possible by the New York State Council
on the Arts with support from Governor Kathy Hochul and the New York
State Legislature. Additional support for Litmus Press comes from the
Leslie Scalapino – O Books Fund, The Post-Apollo Press, individual
members and donors. All contributions are fully tax-deductible.

Catologing-in-Publication Data is available from the Library of Congress.

Litmus Press
925 Bergen Street, Suite 405
Brooklyn, New York 11238
litmuspress.org

Distributed by Small Press Distribution
1341 Seventh Street
Berkeley, California 94710
spdbooks.org

To Mirène Ghossein

PARIS, WHEN IT'S NAKED

When it rains in Paris Europe brings out its umbrellas. Quick, the morning paper is thrown into the basket. Coffee is thick with cream, to make you miss Vienna, and there is a smell of buttered bread on the heavy coats of the men who hurry to their desks. It's dark in the Metro, and messy. There are many young women among the passengers, some of them having never read *Le Spleen de Paris*. Of course, Baudelaire loved London. In the buses, electric bulbs shine, and the morning still looks like the evening before with the same customers who for years still wonder if they should smile at each other. Today's not the day. Those who go to work in their cars carefully wash their windshields, sometimes with a swift stroke of their sleeve. It's very difficult to find a parking place when the weather is poor, which it is most of the year. Some courageous citizens give their dog a morning walk. The people and the animals get wet, but there are unavoidable duties to perform, and they follow the rule. The morning news is all about Europe. European unity is a panacea, and the average Frenchman wants to know how high the snow is in Russia. Maybe, with the fall of communism, winters will be less harsh and the Russian economy will rise. So all kinds of little clouds crowd the

T.V. sets, not only those coming from the Atlantic, but also those from the North Sea. Oh yes! there was a storm over Hamburg. In the meantime, the rain has not abated. You can't see outside, and you can't open your window. It's dark until noon, then it's already late for a good light to fall from the sky. You raise your nose, look at the heavens, and no angel with a trumpet appears. Very ominous clouds cross the sky. They run over each other, they pour. So you listen to the one o'clock news and you know that the races have been cancelled. Again. If you have the radio on, you're told that it's because of the weather; if you have Channel One, or Two, they show you restrained horses wearing blankets. You wonder if these blankets are wet, and hope for the best. Anyway, you don't bet on horses. It's getting late. You don't exactly know late for what, but it's too late. The sidewalks are shiny, and slippery, too. There's water on everything. It's raining all over Europe. In the Italian part of Europe there's a semblance of sunshine. But is Sicily European, really? Are we going to integrate these hot southern countries into our nordic economies? Will it rain more, down there, once Europe gives itself a common army? Nobody has answers for anything nowadays. What if the Russians bring their winters to the western parts of Europe? How are we going to get up in the sheer blackness of Sweden's mornings at the same hours as in Paris? Incredible problems will have to be resolved. Of course, there are the trains. They don't slip on pavements, they don't fear storms. They leave, and they arrive, on time. They're a European invention after all. They suit European weather. Look how well they cross Switzerland with no additional effort! And France will extend the lines of its bullet trains all the way to Spain. Once in Spain, you will see what you can do to stay dry. Look, you can also stay in Paris. The rain washes the monuments carefully, takes the leaves away from the trees, melts itself into the Seine, so you don't know if you're walking, or floating, and isn't this a wonderful state of mind? But it's getting darker, if you can imagine such a thing. Little lights fight their way to your eyes. Oh, yes, you are in the narrow Rue des Canettes, and there is a Greek restaurant with a special container for wet umbrellas, so you won't have to sit on yours, and get arthritis. You go in because you're hungry, and because in Paris there is nothing else to do but eat here and there in all these foreign food places, and they're less boring than the foreign films in the cinemas. Who wants to see on the screen the Moscow Metro when the French ones are inundated! But this particular Greek restaurant doesn't serve Greek specialties anymore, so take your wet umbrella, resume your wet coat, go down the wet street, under the pouring rain, and look for some inexpensive Chinese or Vietnamese eating place. But beware, you're already stepping out of Europe, and Europe is not yet formally founded. You'll have to wait for the end of the year. At least, you're in Paris, and you know it, and it doesn't need Europe, or any other continent. And you will never die of thirst, in this city, as in African deserts; your skin will never

3

dry out, your complexion will remain pleasant. Although you'll never have the pink cheeks of English princesses, unless the Common Market really works. For the time being, try to find some little joint which has a good inexpensive Bordeaux sold as house wine, because rain makes your pocket and your throat feel dry. And then, look at Paris, do it in your imagination if your eyes can't find it, and see what a solid mass of a city it is, what a fugue in its composition, what an epic story in its stones, what an evanescent spirit in its rain.

PARIS, WHEN IT'S NAKED

I had my friend's aunt to lunch. Christmas is three weeks old. Jesus has already grown, and in a few months, before spring's end, he will die. So there is some melancholy in the air, reinforced by the rain. It's raining softly, too softly to matter for the trees of the Luxembourg Gardens, but this rain is steady, and after a while it will be good for French agriculture. It's good for my soul, too, which is in danger of drying up after all the reading of newspapers that I do. I need the rain, and it's here, against my windows. In the meantime, I forgot about my friend's aunt. She did arrive at 1 p.m., with an umbrella. She looked exhausted. After a while we sat at the dining room table. We had to keep the lights on, because it's dark, all day long; of course, at night too, but that goes without saying. I had, for each, a white boudin, a sausage made of chicken and milk. A Christmas tradition for the French. In France, I try to do as French people do. With the boudin come apples, acid, green, Canadian apples, heated with butter. They took time to cook, so the boudin was a bit cold when served. Which is not a traditional way to do things. After the boudin I had a long fish, a "bar." It was fresh, expensive, but it was boiled, and some of its taste was drained out into the soup which we threw away. Out of the 365 varieties of cheese that France can produce we chose three, but no one touched them at lunch. A huge tarte Tatin that I bought on Rue Vavin competed successfully. It was not heated enough, and I was slightly embarrassed. My friend's aunt was in a subdued mood. She ate very little, her wine stayed in its glass. Her melancholy seeped into the room. It was dark in her heart, it seemed. Her children did not spend Christmas with her, nor New Year's eve. They had various engagements in various countries. So she spent her holidays with the memory of her son, the one who committed suicide not too long ago. Her eyes, which are bluish, have a visionary look. Her manner has real elegance. Lavas of affection boil within her heart. But she keeps her emotions to herself, used, as she is, to keep her dignity while letting everybody close to her have his or her own way. She never asked anything, and gave more than she received. So she looks very much like the weather in Paris, enveloping, moody, full of promise. She has moisture in her eyes, a fair complexion, and she doesn't hurry in anything, although carrying great impatience within her, exactly like this season, which is winter, but is readying to explode into an exuberant spring. But the Luxembourg, nearby, is sumptuous, like her, really, in its bareness, because it is reduced to essential forms. You are not distracted by color, or foliage, when you go to meet it, you face a forest of dark columns, tree trunks which stand straight and alive like an army frozen by a camera. Our guest had to leave, and she left behind her a vacancy, an absence, something like questions hanging in the air. She was missed, although she will never know it, or believe it, if we tell her. She is not used to knowing her impact on those who very well know her power to attach people to herself. She sees solitude around her but this solitude is inhabited by the silent passion of those who live close to her. She left behind her like a cloud, like a mist, a perfume made of passing time, a trail of unspoken words. I opened the windows, not knowing exactly what to do, and Paris slid in, filled all the spaces, chilled my face. Then I closed them, bringing in from the balcony a vase full of roses, roses I had received for the holidays, which I drew carefully with Sumi ink, and which I keep out most of the time so that they last longer. But I needed them, their company became essential when I realized that my guest was already back into her home, and that the fog outside had thickened. As I am a news addict, I put on the radio, but they were giving sports scores, and they flashed the name of the German girl who won a championship at Garmish. The snow was not too good, I heard, and at that point I switched off the station. Paris doesn't need me, I felt, I must start considering seriously my way back to California. But an accumulation of reasons keeps me here and now that the afternoon is moving ahead rapidly, I put on my coat and decide to go to the Saint-Claude café. Oh! it's drizzling. As there is melting snow, there is melting rain, drops which do not reach the ground: they seem to evaporate before the end of their course. So I have the feeling that I slide through sheets of water without taking on their full impact. In the café, my friend Claude (no relation with the place), is sitting with a book of poems. We do not say anything special to each other, only that Paris is beautiful. But in that word beautiful there are centuries of lives, of wars, of work, of faith, of deaths. Paris is indeed beautiful, the last of the great cities of the world which has kept its *soul*, which works like a well-oiled machine. Paris is beautiful. It aches to say so, one's arms are never big enough to hug such an immensity. Claude can say it innocently. It's harder for me to say so, it's also more poignant. It tears me apart. Paris is the heart of a lingering colonial power, and that knowledge goes to bed with me every night. When I walk in this city I plunge into an abyss, I lose myself in contemplation, I experience ecstasy, an ecstasy which I know to be also a defeat. Look, look how ugly are the Arab Quarter's pimps, how dehumanized the Algerians who squat in it, how destroyed their women, how degrading their prostitution to the very ones who vote for their expulsion. And I consider this monstrous being called Paris to be beautiful, which it is! It's already late, late to keep sitting in the café. I come back home by some narrow streets, cross Place Saint-Sulpice, and I do it slowly because I love water on water, and it's raining on the flowing fountains. A good winter night to stay home, remember the lunch I had, perplexed, unsure of anything. Then, I'm not sleepy, the hour inside the apartment resembles the one outside, and I don't draw the curtains. I like my shiny black window-panes, and no noise ever comes in from this street. I switch on the 10 o'clock news and, flash! news from the Empire: Algeria's President has resigned to make room for a military takeover against the Islamic parties which won handily their recent elections, because that's also Paris' wish. How can such a huge difference between cultures be tolerated by a dominant power? It would be like forcing Americans to admit that tacos are as good as their morning cereals. French women can bear to know that women in Algeria are starving, but they can't stand the knowledge that these Algerian women say their prayers at home while their French counterparts go to mass. Can a people who think that they practically invented logic be asked to be logical? So in the night, sitting close to my T.V. set, I see tragedy getting ready to unfold. It's too late for phoning anybody, and what can anybody tell me which is not already told? It seems to me that I'm shivering, so I make sure that my bed is made, that the blankets didn't slide away, that there is water left in the bottle of Volvic, and I take my shoes, my socks, my clothes, off, and I get ready, under my covers, to sleep, if I can.

PARIS, WHEN IT'S NAKED

This Algerian thing, for us, here, mostly on television; a decision has been taken to stop the popular will of a country ruined by fraud, turned into a desert by greed, exhausted . . . But I am in an imperial capital, with an inoffensive-looking flag: no eagle on this city's armorial bearings, but flowers; a flower symbolizes France the way the *Flowers of Evil* symbolize poetry. The venomous flowers of Power. We should write that treatise, one day. A long Sunday afternoon of winter is the hardest thing to face, a kind of death in slow-motion, an unmovable boredom, or, worse, an abyss of anxiety. Am I fearing for the palm trees of Biskra? Yes, everything is possible. And going out is so painful, walking in the humidity of this aquatic city. Look: it has fountains, clouds over them, rain between earth and sky, and a very large, a very wet, ancient, river, which here and there splits into a fork, then gathers its waters again, and goes, for ever, to the ocean. When I move through all that, I see myself in one of these movies from the Thirties, when France had not yet been defeated for the third time by the Germans, when it saw itself as fluid power, mercurial

9

empire, lord of the colonies, which also meant rubber and cocoa. But this Algerian turmoil made of France a nation with two faces: one turned East, as under Charlemagne, and one turned South, where its underbelly lies. The cool partners are east of here, where it snows, where one can ski, can warm oneself next to a fire. The dominated live south, where the sun exercises its fierceness; the poor there disturb the rich's warm sleep, they who can break houses with impunity. I'm destined to be on the side of the poor even if I don't want to be poor. The poor can hypnotize the weak, they can bring out the last threads of chivalry in anyone, they can infuriate. I'm on their side for none of these reasons. It is that I got up one morning out of a long sleep, and found myself lying next to them, engulfed by their proximity. If it takes to wrap myself in large sheets of cloth, to go close to them, and feel what they feel, for instance in the streets of Algiers, I will do it. They constitute a forbidden city and if you go on living in the north of the northern hemisphere, you'll have no other way to confront them than from the other side of a gun. You can go on living like a fish in the huge aquarium of Paris, and feel safe, licking with your eyes the windows of pastry-shops. You can also burn, with prayers in the stomach instead of bread, if you go more to the south, and cross the Mediterranean, and stay there, if you so decide. Who among us has such guts? I, for one, don't seem to have them. So I'm chained to my melancholy, which is a sense of helplessness, of defeat, rather than a romantic sadness. In fact, it's the opposite of a romantic state. Nowadays, if one suffers, it is of the drying of one's arteries, or the petrification of the heart. There are also all these considerations that surround you if you live in Paris. People worry about the nuclear bombs that are loose in the former Soviet Union. The Russian fleet has been divided in the Black Sea like spoils of war. The Ukraine has its own admirals. It would have sounded fine in the 19th Century. But we are nearing the 21st with no adequate ideas of how to face it. How can we get ready for a century? It's not a party, after all. We swim in full madness when we think that we have to be prepared for anything. Things make us. We don't make them. The weight of this weather is an element of my soul. Temperatures in their rise and fall regulate or disrupt our heartbeats. I come from very far within to the edge of my own body to meet the sunrise. Oh! it's brief. Then I plunge into that mushy mix of air and pollution, breathe it with variable difficulty. It happens that I remember most of the time, if not uninterruptedly, who I was a few hours, or days, ago. This is reassuring. It allows me to feel and to think. Yes, feelings. They're ideas too, of their own kind. Feelings are antennae, and they open up spaces there in front, not unlike snowmobiles in snowed-in territories. But there is no snow in Paris, not often, not this year. The weather is warmish and wettish. Feet get heavy, backs bend a little, strides slow down. So you think: how quiet can this city get, suddenly, unexpectedly? Buses run empty, so when they go by they don't interrupt the panorama. It's as if nothing happened.

The news-stand is close to the bus stop. I never saw anyone get off the bus just to buy the paper. It will take World War III for that. But you see, European unity is being made to avoid that third W.W. Of course, one never knows, it may very well bring about what it was meant to avoid. 'Europe' is everywhere, most visibly in cafés because you hear people speak Italian, Dutch, German, where you used to hear only French. I am often old fashioned. For example, I love Apollinaire. His *Ballad of the poorly loved.* Am haunted by it. He mentions the London fog, a night in that wilderness, and that double who followed him in lonely places. There isn't enough fog in Paris for committing English crimes. Or English loves. One night I experienced such a total confinement in immaterial matter, such imprisonment in nothing solid, the incapacity to move in total fog being so mysterious, exhilarating, liberating in strange ways. I felt a human form moving in my vicinity, so I called, it was a man's name I pronounced, and in fact it was a young man who answered me, but not the one I thought, and together we moved through invisibility, and we found the door to the student's quarter I was inhabiting. We became very great friends for a very long time.

I thought it would be an enchantment to look at television for the feel of nordic skies, and here is a strike in Marseille which rerouted maritime traffic to Antwerp. What a blessing! I saw huge cranes unload merchandise, but I saw, mainly, the harbor of Antwerp, the sky, a luminous greyness so similar to the painted skies stored in the Louvre. The water, particularly, was flat, and shivering, soft, translucent colors moving gracefully, imperceptibly, on that part of the North Sea which constitutes the harbor. My mind flew, literally. I was floating along seagulls and felt cold, in my apartment, and raised the rheostat. The sky above is grey too but it's a greyness made of metal. Oh Lord! how can we live under so much iron? That carries me back to the situation in Algeria. Why are the roads to popular expression so thoroughly blocked? Why is fear greatest among the most powerful? There is, right now, under the Eiffel Tower, a pitiful protest by young veterinarians whose school is scheduled to be moved into the provinces. 20 students, 5 or 6 dogs, and a full gendarmerie squadron! Poor Mr. Mitterand. He commands a huge army, atomic bombs, a mighty fleet, and he can't sleep because two scores of youngsters who, to make matters worse, *love* animals, are taking a promenade in Paris! Where are we? Couldn't he trust that the rain would break their protest, or the onlookers' boredom? No. The French are getting too serious, which is bad news for Europe. Who is going to be funny, light, in that huge patchwork of nations which is to be completed by the year's end? I would go and buy the afternoon paper but what would it add to the knowledge of the wretched events that occupy our minds? I enjoy the little walks, everything being "little" in this big city. A walk past the Commissariat de police, all the way to the kiosk, after having read the titles at La Procure's windows, which are many in this catholic city-block bookstore: creches, small statues, feathered angels, interfere with the soporific books. Between the Police and the Church (who always lived on good terms with each other), I hurry, regularly, and, at last, I reach the fountain, do my best not to slow my pace near the massive Saint-Sulpice, quickly buy the paper, start to read it on the sidewalk and enter the Café de la Mairie du VIème arrondissement which is part of legends and posterity. You know why. It is the café immortalized by Djuna Barnes, and I dream of her, I say hello to her, every time I enter the café, which is at least once a day. Djuna Barnes. She lived by this fountain, she looked at those maple trees, wrote on these tables, cried on this sidewalk, loved under this weather. There were no Algerian turmoils, then, there were human relations, so to speak, made and unmade love affairs, ecstasy in bedrooms, with curtains drawn, and long shadows, outside, of lovers waiting in the rain. Once, her hotel was the one which is on this square, so she didn't have far to go to reach her café, to maybe smoke a cigarette or two, or go down to 20 Rue

Jacob, where Natalie lived. Oh! I know that courtyard too, I lived on it. But when I fell in love, in there, it was with its linden trees. The difficulties with such a passion were of a different order, not that they weren't tremendous. But tonight, waiting for the rice to cook in the kitchen, I am not quite happy. I talked all afternoon of Marie de Medicis' beauty. It was exhausting. There was also that movie shown nearby of Iraqi children dying from the effects of the continuing blockade imposed on their country. It's too much for a single brain to contain: so many interests, such expansive travels, I mean its thoughts going back and forth in Time. Let's not dwell on this subject: since Saint Augustine nothing has been said on Time that moved us one second on the Great Watch of the Universe. Nothing. So I'm pleased to be indoors, protected from the storm which is bending the Luxembourg Gardens' trees. I know intimately what they're going through. For them, when it doesn't rain, it's worst. Joggers shake their grounds like earthquakes do. I dislike these narcissistic beings who seem to be running after invisible streetcars, never catching one. But life is nice in my neighborhood, even if it's a conspicuously Catholic one. I don't mind it too much. I went to their schools when I was a child. That did not take place in Paris but in one of the then-French colonies. Oppression is very attentive to education. My rice will burn if I don't check on it. It's good to feel hungry, it puts everything into perspective. It's the best antidote to politics. No restaurants for tonight. I don't need to become a cat hunting for a piece of meat or of fish. What shall I eat with my rice? Bread won't do. I got this letter today, from California, telling me that they had a fire in Oakland. It looked like Bagdad, said a fireman, for a while. Well, you can't carry this comparison any further. No. My friend Eric wrote that he made a lot of new paintings. It's good to paint in Marin County. It comes easy. Sometimes goes away easy, too. Who wonders? From where I stand I see many lit windows, and many more which are dark, and in the dark, useless, closed eyes. They're frightening, letting darkness pour into homes, and scary, when the inhabitants are in the country. So many Parisians leave every week-end, punctually, and sometimes for longer periods. The hustle and bustle along the Seine's banks is pushing people to take walks in more peaceful places. Paris buzzes with traffic, proudly so. German cars have not taken over, yet. I should get an East German one, I'm told, they have been forgotten. The German government pays you to get one. What can it do with them? These little machines are eager to roll in Paris, like you, and me, not knowing why.

PARIS, WHEN IT'S NAKED

Something pierced the sky, some light. Clouds flock in from the East. Something both pastoral and epic shakes this morning out of the preceding night. Even the pigeons perch higher, stretch their wings. They are grey, or with white spots, or snow white. When at rest, they wear lacey patterns. Do you think that spring is just behind the door? I don't know. There is something scary in the air, the acceleration of invisible things. I don't see why the asphalt on Rue de Vaugirard, by the Senate, moves the circulation of my blood forward, creates unnameable needs, confuses my will. Its color is silvery and it feels smooth to the eye, and I could faint if I thought about it too long. It curves into Rue de Medicis and the Garden lies there, not the forest it used to be, but a garden, still, winning its fight to retain its mystery. Temperatures are slightly on the rise, with occasional pockets of cold. The chill bites one's ears. Stepping into the street is like washing one's face in cold water. You never experience the feeling of having gone far, in Paris. It's always familiar. The unity of its architecture makes it shrink, because you constantly move between the sumptuous and the intimate. You never fall into wilderness. I look desperately for friendships, otherwise how could I face a city which is a stage for intimacy without meeting someone dear to my heart? Paris is a city for lovers because the decor is here, enhancing love's absence to a maddening degree. Loneliness is therefore, ironically, of the essence of Paris, for no love can fulfill the expectations that the city creates. So, very often, I love the sky, or the rain, or the particular quality of the light that has just disappeared. Gone the celestial lambs and the phosphorescence. Now the sky is functional and my thoughts need redirection. And when you don't know what to do with yourself you turn on the T.V., and turn it off. At this hour, Joan Littlewood is sitting in her apartment, writing her Memoirs. I can phone her and ask the year she is on. I can also try to see her tonight. She was recently in London, trying to ask some of her company's former actors what they still remember, where is so and so, who died recently. Some of these (old) actors come to see her, bringing flowers. I found some of these flowers wrapped in transparent paper, surviving in the sink. We can never have a conversation on the theatre. Never. One day she tells me Shakespeare is no good, another, she recites whole scenes, or even acts, from one of the *Henry*s or from *Macbeth*. Macbeth recurs in her memory. The Macbeths, she calls them. That odious, ominous, couple. Then she reverts to her cockney accent which suits her neighborhood. She becomes stocky, pugnacious, witty, younger than the young. She's a stubborn and arrogant person given to this hunt of the past, she who hates any shred of sentiment. There is a work to be done, of putting on the stage that a piece of paper represents, all these characters who themselves played characters, and who are now coming back, one after the other, to people the vast expanse of her mind. To go and see her, I have to take Rue Soufflot, and go behind the Pantheon, and I dread that mausoleum, the more so since President Mitterand played in it his phoniest act, on his nomination day. Remember, he went into that tomb to salute France's grand men. It worked, for some.

Such a morbid day! Suddenly all the soot on the monuments was visible. The garbage, everywhere. Paris can become a huge kitchen, full of refuse, smelling of grease, steaming. Interrupting my inspection of the sky, the building's architect comes to see me about the neighbor's chimney which leans on the south wall. He's all upset by the state of affairs in France. No. Things can't go on the way they do, he says. Too many immigrants are making the French foreigners in their own land! I see his paranoia enlarge his pupils. I know how he feels. Half-reality, half-myth, immigration is a problem here. The change is too sudden. My architect-friend rambles on. He speaks of absinthe. "You know," he tells me, "absinthe, the 19th Century's essential brew, the alcoholic's ideal drink, the deaths it was supposed to bring in its trail, well, you know," he continues, "in the 3rd Book of the Apocalypse the angel with his trumpet announces the agent for destruction: Absinthe! It is mentioned 5 times! Well, absinthe in the Ukrainian language is the word Chernobyl! Now you can draw the inevitable conclusion of such a revelation. From there, where can you go?" We do go, though, into the heart of France, where we find the most extraordinary stone-built small towns. There, stones write the people's little histories, they are living archives, elements of beauty. Beautiful constructions of the mind house ordinary living. As in Paris, Rue du Parc Royal: there is a rose building, as rose as roses, a dream frozen into stone. To see it I take bus no 96, cross from the Left to the Right Bank, over the

19

Seine, oh the mirror! Is it water that I see, or the water's reflection into water? Does the sky borrow the river's colors, is the river becoming the sky? Are you always 14 years old, just because you live here, not that you're happy, or that 14-year-olds are. But you're stirred by the sun which is red and radiant, which leaves trails of cool fire. You are overwhelmed to see Rome in Paris: these walls of golden stone which trace the tall boundaries of the Seine. A dream of Italy travels perpetually this far north, and the bridges with their soft curves step over the water, symbols of the linkages that will make Europe. Bridges over Spain's torrents, then the ones in Verona, whose very mention illuminates my heart, the ones in Amsterdam. I could count a thousand bridges! And some, or most, of my favorite ones, are right here, and I will go out, right now, and somewhere at the Quai des Grands Augustins, I will cross the River, slowly, looking west, where the sun, had it been visible, would have set.

PARIS, WHEN IT'S NAKED

The news in Paris is always in Algiers. The Algerian junta took over the country's oil, its desert, palm trees, coastal cities . . . French painters haven't gone there for local color for decades. That's gone. The sun moved north, instead; the Tropics are north of Nice. But Algeria, like veiled women, haunts France. They used to love its wines, its very name. Through it they had direct access to Africa's jungles. Gone, all that is gone. France has its seedy politics, too. Now, the rejection of North-Africans is the main issue of French identity. Germany will be Europe's financial power, they say. Italy will produce scholars of Renaissance worth. The French will have to look south, there where mirages pave the desert. You see, when you don't invent religions you take the desert for God, hallucinate from daybreak to dawn, let yourself go thirsty, and brush death with your passage. It could be exhilarating. Otherwise, you're stuck. The news generation is on the go. Everything that happens on the European continent is of serious concern. The Russians are going to church. Where did the monks hide? Were they saying masses in catacombs under the Kremlin? We're presented with empty stores. Did we liberate Russia to look at pictures of emptiness? And where is the Russian soul? Did it get lost? Trusting the latest films I saw at the Cosmos, I wouldn't think so. It's down in Africa that things are disturbing. Is a Moslem soul similar to a Christian one? Should the Pope answer that question? That's the mood in Paris. Is France in danger of disappearing under hordes of Eastern Europeans or will it have to die once more across the Mediterranean? We can't see any further. We're not waiting on the borders to stave off a Chinese invasion. That's America's problem, and anyway not today's. In the meantime the restaurants are full. A socialist government always makes sure that its intellectuals eat out (so they can write all morning). Mitterand himself was a faithful customer of the Balzar where he carefully prepared his ascension to power from behind the white linen napkin that he used to spread over his chest. I never go to the Balzar, or not more than once a year. Rue Racine's restaurants are more fun. The Italian one, specially. I take that street often because it starts at the Odeon Theatre from where you can peek at the Luxembourg Gardens, and read the posters. Most of the plays are in foreign languages, European, of course. Under Europe's unity everybody will become multilingual. Thus Europe will be an intelligent place, which it already is. But it's hard to find a good novel among recent publications. The best books are on Greek philosophy, the Presocratics, I mean. I keep hoping for the discovery of new fragments, uselessly. Still, huge and magnificent works are regularly being written about these incredible texts to which Socrates put a term by his excessive argumentation. Europe knows what it's doing. Let's go back, it says, to where we started, which means to Asia Minor. O Heraclitus! what was the river you knew so well? How did you survive your own impermanence? Can we read you, for sure, through our dark streets and closed horizons? This is why I prefer to close my eyes when I read you, so to speak. Let Heraclitus fill your mind, let your horizon be a burning fire under your eyelids. That's where Greece eternally resides. In the meantime, I'm eaten up by all kinds of little chores buzzing at my ears. Today, I wrote many letters, a long one to Duncan (his eyes always meet the weather) . . . , went to the Post-Office. What a line! Waited for 25 minutes, did not lose patience, gave my letters the way you give a present, or send a child to school, and when I exited, with my letters gone, I felt undressed. It was early afternoon, I had to retrieve a drawing I had bought, took the bus. Hearts are heavy on such days with nothing on the horizon to cheer them. There is always food in Paris, pastry, cheese, paté, but there is a limit to what one can eat innocently. And what about the larger causes for sadness, the ones that never get solved, the territories occupied, the lack of rejoicing in the world at large, the evergrowing quantities of instruments of death, everywhere, absolutely everywhere? When the sky itself reminds us of tanks, when windows in beautiful streets get to be as black as prison-windows, when walls are messy, used by dogs, decrepit, one is really cornered and prone to notice that window frames are indeed black and cold. Is a window meant to keep you in, or open your perceptions to the outside? Windows around stairways belong to the movies world. Look how many ghosts are climbing the stairs, there, on the other side of the courtyard! This will never relieve your anxiety. Anxiety is here to stay.

It's always a matter of weather. Slight pressures of temperature redirect our thoughts. Slightly, imperceptibly, sensations turn into little boats drifting under the breeze's direction. Am I in Tiburon, breathing spray and mist while I know that I'm sitting in the solidity of Paris? Do I know where I am when the heat is even in this apartment which faces walls and windows? While the planet moves since its inception we look for a semblance of stability, making an unforgivable mistake. Oh to keep going! But where to?: on the surface of continents, or back and forth, from the past to the future. We continually miss the mark of the present, the weather's edge. The chase leaves me breathless whenever I dare it. I usually lie on my bed, listening to the buzz in my ears. Everything is still. Dead waters. Suspicious greyness. The rhythm of the metros becomes the city's heartbeat. Every fraction of a second somebody is crying, or shouting his pain, being tortured, selling himself, or dying. So much simultaneity of feelings! Such a river of blood is flowing in Paris, outdoing the Seine, a warm river which invisibly runs in the peoples' arteries. Everything is liquid, our destinies above all. We're at the unknown's mercy. I would rather go out and follow my usual itinerary. The air is cool outside, my skin friendly, not chappy. It's not dangerous to walk without scarves and hats. The coat can stay unbuttoned. There is nothing to beware. You can walk freely up Rue de Medicis, then turn on Rue Auguste Comte. The latter is quite uninspiring. It happens often, in Paris, that a street is no fun even when it touches the most beautiful thing in town, in this case the Garden. Ironies are part of things' lives too, not only of our own. I'm watching the trees change their shades of color and sparrows flutter. I know that in the process I'm ageing, but aren't we trapped in Time and obliged to follow its course, to become one with it? A slight wind has raised dust. Paris is a seashore town, but the sea receded millions of years ago. The sand has remained. The Atlantic used to blow its waves here. There is some salt still in the air, in spite of the lead that we breathe. It's quite an odyssey to turn in circles in a section of the same arrondissement: you either encounter centuries fixed in stones, or people from all the lost civilizations of the earth. Some sit in a café and let their mind empty itself; it's like servicing one's car, regularly. Then, when they speak, it's like they are talking to gods. But I don't want any of that. I love my near-misery. It's a response to what shakes the Heat Belt: Down there, in Algeria, south east of here, in Egypt. I have a strange contract with these countries. I'm called, and never go. The sirocco is soon to be blowing. The wind will throw handfulls of sand into peoples' eyes. Here it will be muggy, thick, a thick air will call for rain. The wind will pass through shutters in horizontal sheets and keep going. It will cease to be French and become a European wind. My shutters stay open. If I had to close them I would leave this city. Nobody asks me any report on my activities, or my condition. My windows are my dearest property given that we live in cages. It's not because our walls are lined with books that we're not encaged, nor because we think that it's all a matter of free choice. I see homeless people carry cardboard boxes with a sense of discovery that millionaires have when they buy huge apartments on the Champs-Elysées. But the former will get colder in them, in their cold misfortune, while the latter . . . well, we know too much about the latter. A strange taste of bread and butter is lingering in my mouth. The café au lait was not enough for my morning thirst. I'm going to wear my other clothes, the ones for the street, those which make up for lost heat, and go to my daily hunt, where I can eat a bit better than yesterday, or in a place less crowded with noise than the Chai de l'Abbaye, less expensive than Leonora's. For everything, there's a decision to be made: to declare a war, or buy a piece of soap, the mental operation is the same. The results, too. After all, aren't wars a cleansing operation?

PARIS, WHEN IT'S NAKED

I will go on, collecting perceptions. If Paris were a deadly poison, I would have gladly drunk a big portion, and silenced my life. But this is a daily poison, minute drops of arsenic, a distilled evil, a passionate addiction. I am an adhesive tape on Paris' skin. There are too many people for anyone to be needed. Keep your illusions, though. There. The clock is ticking. My stomach too. A dismal day for going out. But the inside and the outside look more alike than one knows. I know it too well for my own good. I scratched off all kinds of differences for too long a time. Now I'm paying. That payment's modalities have become my own definition. I am what I pay. Why is Richard Brautigan staring at me? I didn't kill him. He did it himself. I never met the man, have only known somebody who knew him. That doesn't make us former friends. And still, he's looking at me. Where's Bolinas? Yes. I'm asking too, echoing his voice: where? I am on the beach at Bolinas smiling, as usual, at the horizon. The waters are iridescent. That's the Pacific, guys! That's not the River Seine. And between the Pacific and the Seine I am at dead center. Facing a decision. Should I go on living in this paleness, under the shadow of French trees, walking painfully? When everything pulls you apart, you play dead. Don't you? Tell me. Who can answer, where are the beliefs of my ancestors? Who were they, anyway? Breathing painfully. Let's open the windows even if they hang over hell. A whiff of cold enters swiftly. One is better outside. And it's lunch time. Past the time. I hurry to Café Rostand. Sitting comfortably, I face the Garden. Yes: ham and cheese sandwich, a squeezed orange. The trees are in front of me, just across the street, tall, showing their stumps. Above them the sky is both luminous and impervious. Nobody today can penetrate its secrets. As I don't have much to do, my mind wanders around. I am not androgynous any more. Androgynes die young: they're ephemeral flowers. When considered a boy, they disappear in the Bois de Boulogne. Some pimp gets their skin. If they were little girls to start with, they die before their first abortion. We have to know it, while the Luxembourg's dark trees repeat Clytemnestra's gesture of impotence in the face of the gods. No it's not going to rain. I better go home. I cross the garden which has open spaces, look at the Medici Fountain, always in the shade, and go toward the little restaurant which hides there, pretending to still be a tea-room. Hello! says Max. I'm sorry, I won't stop, and I will skip the little game he ordinarily plays. Max pushes you to order a lot. He pushes his little grain of sand. No. He is not Sisyphus, he doesn't take himself that seriously. He pushes the bill up a few more francs, and even then he gives you something in return. Not like these lofty Greek gods! But I'd better hurry. The garden is barren; its statues command more attention than its maples, or linden trees. If the trunks were larger they would have looked like wine barrels and put us in a hilarious state. I am not going to start worrying about French agriculture. The new Europe will settle every possible question. You know, some infallible entity is being born under our eyes. Not a revolution. A creation. The greatest creation since the Babylonian Deluge. Switzerland will move closer to Paris, and Berlin, to Prague. We're changing geography, around here. Americans better take notice. But where are the Americans? They left, they tell me, with Voyager 2. They're always in outer space, or spaced-out. They don't rush to Paris, they have been replaced by Rumanians, it seems. If in the markets you listen to all the foreign accents, no American house-wife emerges to your attention. There are new languages in the world and their ambassadors are all here. Paris is always first choice. I did something this afternoon that worries me more than the whole of World History. I went to visit my friend Salma with a house-warming present. When she opened her package I blushed to the very roots of my hair. Good Lord! I picked up the wrong package, I was giving her something rather embarrassing. She said she loved her present. I could not say a word. The afternoon was funny; it went away quickly, and I told her that big clouds were gathering, the bells of Saint-Germain were tolling, so I had to be home before the downpour. In fact, it didn't rain. It was a false alarm, as during the war, when the airplanes were not showing up. The concierge is waiting. When I don't tip her, she tells me awful stories about the civil war in Spain, when her father who was a Catalan republican was forced to march from Barcelona to Paris, on foot, sleeping in abandoned barns, and looking for Picasso. My father searched for me all his life, she says. And as she doesn't say more on the matter I don't press her with questions. Her husband could have been considered to be an Algerian traitor: he fought with the French against his own people. Otherwise, he's nice. Too polite, one day, almost rude, another, apologizing each way. They make me feel slightly sad, don't know why. When I have encountered them I notice that I turn on the T.V. quicker than usual.

PARIS, WHEN IT'S NAKED

Is there any use in watching two pigeons on their way to the zinc at the roof's edge? But if all the day's tiny events were abolished one after the other, I'll end into insanity. Then, new events will rise, more chaotic, very likely more fluid, more turbulent. It's better to admit that the brain is a sleepy fellow, a machine working at one per cent. Not a courageous one, of course. I would rather trust the fig tree in the courtyard next to mine. It is already trying to shake the winter off. Its buds are premature. I can tell their impatience. Being surrounded by straight, lifeless, buildings, it puts up a good fight. I will write an elegy for it, someday, I hope not too dark a day. The chimneys of my neighborhood don't seem to be working. This central heating business has levelled off the temperatures within the apartments. No one can guess the month, the day, the hour . . . you need crutches to know what time it is, buy the paper to know where you stand with the calendar. Yes, Saint-Sulpice's bells are ringing, but what do they say? Nothing. They insist on ringing. That's okay, okay for a while.

We're approaching lunch time. What a bore, this cycle of food. Little crabs, on the beach, don't tire as much as I do. They have different eating habits. Their backs are gently stroked by the sunset's last rays. A wave, so similar to a lip, covers them. Gently, too. And then night falls on the Pacific and an immense roar advances from the beginnings of Being. Here in Paris, Time is older, nine hours older, and its already dawn, a grey dawn, a yawn, a timid sun, and buses grinding their wheels on old avenues. People, all over, eternally hurrying, thinking about their evening meals, their bills, their mistresses. There's a school in my street and children jump, run, walk, pirouette, loaf, dressed in basic blue. Once in a great while a blind man settles at the corner of the intersection and plays waltzes on his mechanical piano. The children gather around him, cheerful, one of them gives a penny, and school is forgotten! I see parents come and spoil the scene. Do parents ever do anything else? A new day brings its harvest of bad news (bad for whom?). What's going on in Washington? Now that Iraq is thoroughly mowed down we can always presume the next target's name. Are we going one day to destroy countries because they play poor football, boot them out of this world because they took possession of some materials lying under their grounds? God knows what's coming! Yes, there are too many people on the planet, so the question will soon be: which nation ought to disappear to make room for which other? The fact that this has already happened doesn't guarantee us a safe future. So if my horizon is so foreboding, what shall I do? The papers say that there are a few movies one should see. I can take a walk (like a dog would do), stretch my legs, draw a circle with my steps. Inevitably, I will be back at the Odeon Theatre. Inside, everything is claustrophobic: a closed stage for a closed space. Few plays break its boundaries. Instead of going there I'll go out on my small balcony (yes, in big cities everything has to be small). The sky is uncertain, washed out, a piece of tired linen. It's cold, everything is wet. I carefully come in, close the door behind me, and sit on the couch. There isn't much to think about, for me, right now. Every avenue of thought leads to some disaster. There are apples in the Portuguese ceramic plate, silent and friendly. Counting apples doesn't cure my heart's sickness. What powers do I have? Let's take a breather and answer this fundamental question. None, is the reply. Almost none. Absolutely no power. Can I meet Monsieur Mitterand to tell him who is dying where, why, and for what? Certainly not. Can I visit the Chief Justice of the Court in The Hague to ask him to study the merits of some Liberation Front? Am I kidding? Can I prevent the felling of trees which makes room for tennis courts on the Luxembourg's sacred grounds? No one even bothers to make fun of my proposition. But chunks of freedom are available: look, I can buy coffee or tea, go or not go to the movies, I can, I . . . this game creates hardship to my head and I have to give it up. It has been a long day, nothing changed in the courtyard, nobody opened any windows, so no windows will have to be closed, and I'll have to go to bed, because that's what's done during these late hours when the theatres are closed, the metros stopped, and the police, dozing. I think the fountain stops at night, too (not out of its own free will). The pigeons sleep on the shoulders of stone (and famous) cardinals. I will not disturb them with my thoughts. Jacob, nearby, fights his angel, day and night, like me. He does it not in the desert, but in Saint-Sulpice, a good place to look for angels. And in Delacroix's painting God watches in the form of an omnipresent tree. There are many angels around me. My enemies belong to angelic orders, I mean, the dark ones. They come at night, carry my bed into the courtyard, and when they're sure I'm in great discomfort they bring me back. I make them believe that it all happens in my sleep. In the morning I find messages from them by my door. The concierge keeps telling me that these were in the mail. Maybe. I seldom receive any good news in the mail. How can I? I'm not going to tell where all these letters come from. There is unity in some peoples' lives. A Frenchman in Paris watches French variety shows. To my life there is no such center. I borrowed the French language (it was decided for me, I should say), borrow their city, buy Yugoslav shoes, Scottish cashmere sweaters, Italian socks (like all of you). I'm not going to carry this any further lest I discover that my cells are made of Argentinian meat and Dutch milk.

Definitely East, Paris is looking. A love affair is developing with the Russians, an old passion revived. A cascade of movies is descending on the movie-halls, Saint-Petersburg has had a lovely autumn, the Moscow Philarmonic plays Tchaikovsky (on T.V. alas!). You would think that Boris Yeltsin single-handedly created all this cultural richness in about a year . . . In the meantime many countries are dropping out of History. The faster the better. I can see the new world order becoming a new Columbus expedition. We already know the results. Yes, Paris is an aquarium because you move within it with your fins and feelers. You never find what you think is there. Walking in the streets, you could literally be in a series of innocent villages. And still, much hatred is living here, always in the name of reason. The most dangerous people are the journalists: whoever arouses their anger is lost to posterity. Paris loves to appear frivolous. It's ruthless, but the hammers are covered with furs. Somebody offered me a number to call on the Minitel: pornography with a sweet voice. Selling women is part of the freedom of expresson and of a market economy. If it happened in Africa, Western generals would arrive in their trucks. Of course, if they did it there, it would be at least in a real market place shimmering with the smell of desire. They will not do it, though, but the generals can still take a trip . . . one never knows. Africa haunts Paris. Immigration is an ominous question which makes France run on differing logics. Political posters belong to the realm of fiction. They're tempered by those who advertise cultural activities. Last year, it was the centennial of Rimbaud's death. Imagine! He must have turned over in his grave. Literati used him for their personal project. There was even a caravan of poets mocking (?) his peripatetic life. I had to stay distant from his work, feeling that it needed a vast area of silence to recover. But who can stop literary celebrations in such a literate capital? This year, we're tackling Stendhal, and before the year is over not a drop of blood will be left in his arteries. Poor Stendhal! My head hurts when I try to see through the haze. We act on so little knowledge; I would rather swim across the English Channel on a night of total fog. Oh the blessings of fog! It provides the only time when people admit that they can see nothing! What a beauty in that certitude. A rest. The purification of the heart. But I'm not in the Alps, French or Bavarian, I'm in a city with long historical continuity, sure of itself, meddling with everything, allowing (although in a diminishing way) everyone to pursue his folly. Today, for example, there will be a march against the hunger imposed on Iraq. What good will it do? Banners will float under the resisting sun, the mist is lifting, a handfull of people will carry their will to the streets. Yesterday, it was the medical employees who were marching. Tomorrow, it will be the potato growers. So there are long promenades and onlookers pressed against café windows. An atmosphere of fanfare overtakes the city.

It's nice. The feast is always where the unhappiness lies. Which makes me desirous to use the time machine backwards and go to Catalonia, in 1937, alongside the Passionaria, and believe in the possibility of freedom. I can't believe in much, right now, save in the suffering of peoples, yes, but that's not a belief, it's a fact. I don't see my way in that tunnel. You don't resolve problems, in Paris, you chat, you measure the extent of your powerlessness. That's what it means to be marginal. Everybody, besides a few thousand, is marginal, in Paris. It all creates a fever, a maddening desire with no object, special ways of walking, hollow cheeks, beautiful eyes. You can vote, of course, but for whom? You can go fishing, which is more substantial. More costly, too. I used to fish in the Seine, a few decades ago. But where have the fish gone since those shimmering days? Memory is like this river, full of dead bodies, but nonetheless flowing to where the ocean lies, and the breeze. My heart is tight with apprehension, and I received many blows, on the crowded sidewalks, this afternoon. As it is Saturday, Parisians go shopping, and the overflowing goods they buy make them look ugly. I fear to become what I see: patches of black color, rotting plastic bags. I know that they don't rot, but they do, becoming pitiful and dusty. I don't want to be all the shoes at André's, all the little bottles of perfume on Rue du Vieux Colombier. I'd rather not be. And who wants to become a bus? This winter is peeling the calendar's leaves. It did not bring special happiness to the pigeons and is fast joining the millions of nondescript winters that went by since the earth began spinning. There were a few I loved. Not this one with which I don't seem to communicate. It's too warm in the apartment, luke-warm. A last peep of light is showing through the curtains. My thoughts tune themselves to the ambiant temperature. I would have been ashamed if anybody cared. At least, I don't have a dog.

PARIS, WHEN IT'S NAKED

The temptation is to get out of here. Such a force of gravity exercises itself on this city that one can sit on a chair and many years later find oneself still sitting and ageing. Where to go, where? Once in the air a plane has the infinite to itself, but we're not flying that high, we're not free. Free as a bird. What an illusion! The birds of Paris seldom leave the plazas or the courtyards in which they are born. Yet they do give some sense of freedom, which shows how trapped we are. Confinement is the human condition. Let's face it. A few people manage to widen their horizons. Ansel Adams comes to mind. And that could be another illusion. It's a bad day for freedom. I don't have to close my eyes, the sea is in front of me most of the time, regularly. It is open on each side, and all the way to the horizon. The horizon used to be my childhood home. I know it so well. I built on it complete cities, surrounded by flames, and they were engulfed in fires like the city of Smyrna in the early twenties. While they were dancing in many world capitals, all kinds of vessels were carrying the fleeing people of Smyrna to new destinations. The Greeks kissed Anatolia good-bye. And the sea is all over, with long trails of fiery reflections, and we are criss-crossing in a small embarcation. From Paris you can tell that History is full of negative energy, live wires sparkling in Chaos. All you need to recreate this intensity gone is to enter into these fabulous and dusty bookstores, things like Maisonneuve and Samuelian, always located on narrow sidewalks with water running in the gutter. This is a good place to travel without buying tickets, queueing at airports. The corner of one's eye catches hundreds of book titles, each an invitation to a voyage. Coming out, little illuminations accompany me for a while. I have to say that in my neighborhood when not on Saturdays, I can walk in the middle of the road and it is seldom that a car chases me away, after having chased a pigeon or two. Rue des Canettes bewilders me the most. Is it narrow or large, crowded, or quiet, wet, or dry, reeking of beer, or wine? There are streets which keep you guessing. From here, I go and sit in the Café de la Mairie du VIème arrondissement, smell fried eggs, beer and lemonade, absorb the smoke of the clients, drink a thick coffee, read a stuffy paper like Le Monde, and, oh yes! and think of Djuna Barnes like the first astronaut thought of the universe in the first mongolfière. We have ways, like angels do, of being ubiquitous, we experience ecstasy in the shoddiest places. This Café de la Mairie is not shoddy: it has a rhythm of change which is fascinating, never frantic, never too slow. You think people are revolving, coming at assigned times, moving happily, contemplating glasses which catch the subtle light of Paris as if it were a message of love. I can't look at the sea, at this moment; my mind has stretched to its limits. Does the mind breathe, like the lungs do? I should say it does. I remember the day by the ocean, in Pebble Beach, when my mind swelled; balloons were popping in my head, my thoughts suffered marvelous distortions. Connections were distended. Two and three made seven, or eight, an object started as a spoon and ended up a refrigerator. The idea of God was most affected: it shrank, God appeared as a point, then the point seemed too big, diluting God's grandeur. I was running after that point and it was receding, until it disappeared in the circonvolutions of my exhausted brain. Paris is neutral grounds. Its revelations are reasonable. A Napoleonic capital is as clear as a map: everything is chartered. The best police system in the world can turn your dreams into a psychological profile. An imperial capital can allow itself thousands of trees with a lot of shade, having weathered the onslaught of world history. It is neither a scared place nor a scary one. The buildings are here to stay. There are old ladies, old enough to be beyond ageing any further. They are angular, too, and cannot be hugged. They are nobody's grand'ma. Childless women come to Paris. The city matches the uninhabited vastness of their hearts. However, no apocalyptic wind blows over the city. There is a semblance of normalcy when you think of the rest of the world. It could be that things are not that normal. There's impatience in the air, an urge to shake this society out of its apparent complacency, out of its density. The storm is not in the skies but underground. They may kill the happiness they're enjoying. Something may go astray. Paris is not fond of earthquakes. It's rather sinking in sand. But its belly can still spit a lot of fire. I see signs of it. The violent sexual images that used to litter the city's walls have quieted to an insipid dullness. There is nothing explosive to be seen. Things exude a slow decay, albeit a controlled one. Stairways, window shades, wooden floors, deteriorate and are swiftly replaced, people being still afflu-ent. But something is eroding, which nobody replaces with spare-parts, some form of what is called "honor" is lacking, more and more, the way food is missing in the supermar-kets of Russia. Around here food is not missing, there is even too much of it, but something dear to the heart, to the mind, is getting scarce, and cannot be imported. Parisians will laugh it off. They are prone to suspicion, fear, resent-ment, regardless of their ethnic background, color, or creed. I can smell it. I do my best to pretend that I don't see it, because I would rather avoid being a target for anything. And that's dangerous too. When something is targeted it ignores it; when at last, or by chance it learns it, it's always too late. Clocks never go back to their early innocence.

There is mistral and tramontana in the Midi. I was going to Nice this morning but I got up after 10 and thought I'll catch the 4 p.m. plane. My legs felt heavy, and the sky darkened. There was no eclipse of the sun, but just the same, something dark was descending on Earth. I thought of the wind: what if it shook the plane and passengers got nauseated. A little walk would take care of my disappointment. It is Sunday, the stores are closed, there won't be traffic outside. I did go down this dismal Rue Madame and turned left, and left up Rue de Rennes. It started to rain slow and heavy drops of water. I met a poet who lives up the street and works as a guard in the museum. His long white beard gives him a pathetic look. He's going to be within four walls in Beaubourg until late tonight. This week he's stuck with Max Ernst. I couldn't help him in his melancholy, the more so that he won't accept long discussions. He tells me to beware words because they easily change meaning and create harrowing misunderstandings. Let's shoot arrows, then. Where are the cafés where we can play such games? The ones I know best are in small California towns, hidden in foothills. Forget it. Face the stillness that surrounds you, the silence, the lack of telephone calls, the darkness. I was going to buy a house in Nice. A balcony, more than a house. A balcony on the sea. The idea is so appealing that I purposely missed the plane.

And I'm going to be so busy that it might never happen. The most beautiful balcony in Nice may very well belong to somebody else. The sea will roar in my absence. I will hide my tears. Other breakers are waiting for me, an undertow of anxiety. How can I let myself go into an oceanic happiness, face an incantatory bliss in front of the sea when I know that so many immigrant workers face possible deportation? You can see Paris with French eyes, fear the influx of the poor from all the continents, see a whole social equilibrium be disrupted. You can also see the immigrant as a human being who happens to be here, now, and imagine the unbearable pain he would feel if he had to leave this little job he has, in the Tunisian grocery store, in the Cambodian's laundry, in this city where men and women learned to drink wine with their bread and cheese, and appreciate the freedom that they seem to breathe. The problems of the future are becoming a haunting reality. Rallies show the rise of intolerance and the arrogance that comes with it, which makes even more disarming the visible satisfaction of the Arab and Black African workers who enjoy such things that we overlook, such as the running of the trains on time. Even the garbage collectors feel proud to be part of a well functioning machinery, with the medical-looking gloves that they have to wear. In no cities of the world can workers be as beautiful, coordinated, urbane, as they are in Paris. I hear them chat under my windows. There is no place that foreign workers would like to go to more than Paris, with its beat, its legend, its traditions of labor unions and admiration for the *travailleurs*. So fanaticism looks out of place, here, although it's becoming part of daily life. Paris weighs on me with all its mass. The different threads which make it up can hardly be sorted out. Swallow your medicine in one gulp, my mother used to say. But when the rain is so persistent, although very light, this year, my mind furiously runs towards distant places. *Anywhere out of this world,* says Baudelaire. The poet of Paris had to get away the farthest possible into the unknown. If only paradise existed for sure! Then it would be only a matter of patience. Sometimes, though, I yearn for a paradise I can experience here and now, and, to be honest, I had glimpses of it in Baja California. I'm ensnared by geometry, architecture, and a river which gives life to all these stones. I'm caught in a language used by Montaigne, perfected by Racine, perverted by Mallarmé into an explosive beauty. I can speak to a real poet named Albiach who is the heir to that great tradition, and still, there is this pain which comes from other places and gets enmeshed in the Raison d'Etat and policies of France. A sandstorm in the Sahara throws its grains into my eyes. A political prisoner in Syria begs for my attention. I can bring him no water, no consolation. This is all part of my living here, while the bells of Saint-Sulpice unleash their call.

Paris: sitting in a storm's eye, with placid self-confidence, repeating its age-long gestures the way old people still get up in the morning like they did when they were children. Paris is no child. It looks soft, non-commital, but hides in its bowels an iron will. It's not going to be submerged by Europe, not going to yield its rank to the Italians, be bullied by the Americans. When speaking to its former colonies, it shows a nordic visage. When dealing with the Anglo-Saxons, it reverts to its mediterranean culture, mixing seduction with ruthlessness not unlike our (unrealistic) image of what we call banana-republics, but with much more affluence, and much less nakedness in its use of power. There's so much firmness in the smallest notice from the Post Office or any of the Ministries that I instantly understand what the gulag must have been. There are no gulags, of course, around the corner, but something tells you that anything can happen while in the same time something else in you lets you believe that nothing of that sort should ever be feared. But in the suburban cafés the fear of deportation is growing, expressed in whispers and rumors. It's a contagious fear, an underground stream of dirty water. Already backs are hunched around a story-teller, and instead of looking at the sky for the sun, workers look at the policemen who drive their cars with subversive nonchalance. Clusters of people wait at street corners, all over town, for the traffic lights to change, they exude quiet determination, but when you address one of them you discover abysses of terror. Oh! little terrors, most of the time. They worry about not finding a ticket for the concert, missing the last métro, by the Bois de Boulogne, or not having change. But they also fear to have their rent raised, their job cancelled, their bank go bankrupt. Adding these worries up creates an ominous dread. I often have coffee with immigrants, unfortunately not Tunisian or Moroccan workers but with wealthy Lebanese who waited for so long for the end of their war that they lost any normal sense of time. I speak with Greeks, Turks, who have a way of narrowing their eyes that touches my heart. Where are the secret beaches of Turkey when we breathe so many fumes, where the sun? I'm condemned to hear their innocent dreams. Proud to be in the last of the great cities of the world, they're not sure that the price they're paying is worth the trouble. They have not many reasons to stay; they have even fewer to go back. In some former centuries they would have made ideal sailors. The rain has stopped, which is scary. The sky is dirty blue linen, the trees are black sticks, purposeless, standing prisoners. Time feels stilled. A pigeon cut the air from one wall of the courtyard to the other. You could have tended a rope under its path. Your vision is horizontal. The different objects of the house get singled out, solitary, like in a painting. Where is the flow? The spring? The estuary? Could tears be dry? Could a whole continent be reduced to a lack of space? Dismal is this season of nothingness. It's hard to see the sky of Paris, I mean when you don't live in certain apartments which are out of your price-range. Some rare evenings, the glow is so strong that a pink hue, an after-hue, an illumination made of color and fire, seeps between the buildings, these evenings which are an illumination for the whole body, not only the eyes. This evening was one of them, and while I looked like any of the women who pass by, carrying biscuits, milk, coffee and croissants, I have been inhabited for a while by such a revelation of cosmic beauty that I felt—at last—that I would be able not to spend all my life (i.e. what's left of my life) in this city. There are negative forms of happiness and such a one followed my exaltation. Haven't you been to the doctor and after he told you that your sickness was incurable but not mortal haven't you felt younger and full of projects? I had a long conversation at noon with my friend Francoise about the Island of the Réunion. It was interesting to hear about it in the small and crowded restaurant called Le Petit Saint-Benoît. Now, after the few minutes of enchantment created by the state of the sky, I will go to that island, some day, some time, after having gone to all these places I keep thinking about, and that will need so much effort, and, mainly, so much time, so much time for Greece, and Turkey, and the Sahara, and the Andes, or at least Guatemala, that it may never be, never. And so will it be.

When the sun itself, in all its torrid glory, does not succeed in warming the earth, the human mind accepts defeat. A cold wind blows across the soul and while the light ascends gradually over the land, a darkness of another nature envelops us. In sheer daylight I cannot find this soul of mine and my demeanor must show the strain under which my life is led. The connections between the hours of the day and those of my inner clock are becoming loose and it won't be impossible that soon they break apart. It is cold. The temperatures are sub-freezing. The metaphors of hell and paradise lose their potency. The day passed indifferently. Not even phone calls brought any surprise. It has been a routine of steps taken within the apartment, of a few elevator rides, a few street blocks to buy coffee, a few others to see a friend in need of money. Some reading was done: a few paragraphs from the beloved Eduardo Galeano. And then, the cold was so strong that I had to hurry back. But before going to bed, I opened the door to the balcony, and looked up the street, first, to my right, then to my left. It was extremely cold. I hesitated before coming in and closing the door. I looked up, toward the sky, without giving much thought to what I was doing. Something shone, sparkled. Good Lord! I saw stars! There *were* stars in Paris's very high sky, I don't remember having ever seen them over this city, ever. And tonight, they're as visible as in a desert sky, they're feeble and cold, they shine persistently, they carry my mind into their crisp world, making me turn with them in a space infinitely colder than mine. Will I put this cold temperature to some use, plunge into a book, acquire, for a few hours, some poet's company? I have tried it, already, with Dante's *Divine Comedy*. The work is too long for my present impatience. I would love to take a train to Italy, go to Verona, rent a room at the Manzini for a month or two, and there read the *Comedy* with interruptions only my own. Would that do? I yearn not for the work itself but for Botticelli's illustrations. I want to read the *Comedy* through Botticelli's soul, see it through Botticelli's eyes, read his lines the way a blind person reads Braille with his or her hands. Where are the original drawings? How can I find them? A new hunger is churning in my stomach. My heart is beating hard. How can I trace these images I saw once, only once, reproduced in book form. I don't have the book anymore, it has disappeared. No poet's verses can right now be tuned to my heart's particular trembling. We should become a single piece of music created by two instruments. Who could be that other instrument I'm looking for? It could be Hölderlin. Maybe. There's a distance between where I stand and where he lies and I can't walk it right now. I'm searching for a poem by Ibn al-Fared. If I find it soon enough, read his mixing of divine love with sexual desire, and the metres of his verse, a kind of accelerated camel's stride, I can probably get out of the dispiritedness in which I'm flexing my wings, trying to fly. Yes, if I want to move toward a kind of sleep which is the mind's real rest, that hour when the sun filters through our eyelashes and the body stretches like a cat's, I will read a few lines, a few pages, then realize that I had gone into a blessed terrain and that my landing was a reassuring one. I'm going to the Luxembourg's octagonal basin. Doves are walking on its frozen surface, and a pale, rose-wood colored sun, with some light left to it, is being reflected. On that narrow luminous trail other birds are walking. Paris is receding North as do its sister-cities of Berlin and Warsaw. Everything southern is kept at bay. We're at the beginning of some private ice-age, the somnolence of winter will conduct us into the northern fields of solitude, where we will forget the interplays of life and death and subsist in darkness, on very little, indeed, very very little.

PARIS, WHEN IT'S NAKED

And so, it's cold. Not as much as in the Southwest, though. The Pyrénnées' foothills are without electricity. Route Nationale 9 is closed. The lack of heating causes worry. What about the old people snowed in? Paris is spared those difficulties. In a sense, it's too bad. A good snow would have changed the landscape. I remember Paris under snow: it's an enchantment, worthy of Saint Petersburg. The black tree trunks against the whiteness! New lines appear, new shapes. No, it's cold today, but in a dull way. I noticed a woman promenading her dog this morning. She wore thick whitish stockings, an old fur coat made of three pieces, a woollen, knitted hat. But, strangely enough, she wasn't wearing gloves. Her dog's leash was rather long. Her animal, a snautzer, I think, wore a coat made of a piece of dark leather. He also wore a fur collar, a lively brown collar. Like in the Dutch paintings in the Louvre. Only that in the Louvre, the collars are made for people and with white lace. The dog's collar was the liveliest thing I saw in the street. It gave me a lift; then I continued to the Flore where a nice, good-looking journalist interviewed me on Lebanon for his radio program on France-Culture. Lebanon looked far away, and almost unreal, seen from the Flore's second storey. I told him that I couldn't speak much about it with the greyness outside and the insipid columns of the *Herald Tribune* in front of my eyes. These American journalists, seen from Paris, seem as pompous as the French ones do, read in Washington. They keep telling their President what to do, and it's always, unmistakably, WAR. The French newsmen use more subtlety. They have a monopoly on moral thinking. I have to order my café-crème. The garçon comes and we shake hands. He's broody. One night he told me, because I was sitting, perchance, next to a famous and incredibly handsome Russian-born actor, that he had gone to drama school with him. The theatre celebrity was an incurable alcoholic; my waiter looked healthy, but they both looked sad and resigned. I had stayed longer than usual, that night, at the Flore. Until closing time, I think. Paris was shiny. Space, above it, looked unfathomable. Paris was under infinity. The actor, the garçon, and I, found ourselves on the same sidewalk, close to a tree. Then our ways parted. Today I left about twelve fifteen. I waited for the green light, crossed the boulevard, reached the Drugstore Saint-Germain, and went up Rue de Rennes, to get lost in an ordinary afternoon. I remember that I have to take the metro to the 16th arrondissement and bid farewell to a Turkish princess leaving for Eastern Russia. Yes, titles are making a come-back. Things have changed. It's to Teheran that one can't go easily nowadays, a place I could have reached by bus from some market place in Damascus. Now some people go to Nijni-Novgorod searching for Michel Strogoff. What happened between 1917 and 1990 east of Poland? We don't know. And with rain pouring down all I want is to avoid the flu, and it feels comfortable to be sitting on Kenize's couch, facing trees. In her microcosm, a series of small gardens becomes a park, a park in Paris easily becomes a private empire. We speak of Turkey, lightly. We complain about the French Left while admitting uneasiness about the future. This is a no-man's-land of a conversation. We speak of the falling of an airplane, two days ago. It looked clumsy and old, lying on the ground, at the end of its rope, like this century itself. I'm leaving this charming little place for the métro, again. The métro turns out to be an underground library: the guy sitting next to me is reading Albert Camus, the girl in front is reading Henry James, in French, a young man is reading on marketing. Further up a passenger is reading something I can't see, and another is scribbling on a pad. I have not run into readers in years. Is this a new city, with people reading at 7 p.m. so seriously, so quietly? Have I been out of touch with things? When I come out at Mabillon Station, having taken the escalator, the familiar griminess reassures me. The sky, if it's there at all, is very low. Two homeless men shout insanities to each other. I'm sorry. I don't know. I'm eager to be home.

PARIS, WHEN IT'S NAKED

I was trying this morning to figure out how one could think without words. A noble desire, I thought. I wanted to get close to what I presume could be forms of animal thinking: what happens in a cat's brain when a cat decides between jumping and not jumping? Does his whole body think? Does the cat compare actual with remembered distances by acting out, within his muscles, the jumping? I tried to stop this inner language that keeps rolling like a reel, and something else stopped, too. I faced blank space. I stared intensely at the windows across the courtyard, moved my eyes north, south, sideways. I found myself stroking walls with my glances and establishing no connections. I became a pure vision of surfaces. I couldn't decide between getting out of my chair, or staying; I didn't make comparisons, either. I stopped recognizing objects as such. Started to fight somnolence. My ears felt heavy. No animal ever experienced such a state, I'm sure. I don't suppose that I'll try again to *be* an animal. It's a lost key for us. We separated ourselves from them. We know that once we formed a single family. But when I tried to put words aside, for good, I ended in a painful state of being: surfaces hypnotized me, and, in front of an orange, I didn't know how to behave. An orange patch of color located itself in a round shape, shape and orange disappeared into a continuum, and I slept soundly. No, that was not a successful morning: a cream-colored universe surrounded a dozing figure, and time went by, unwitnessed, as I realized later. When I woke up, it was one of these dim afternoons when Parisians turn on their electric lights just after lunch. A whitish sky was covering us all and some of that whiteness was running over the buildings. It was a good moment to think of death. Death looked like a world with no words. Something pure, made invisible by its absoluteness. It occurred to me that the cruellest thing that God inflicted on us was immortality. "You shall never die" God must have said in the Gardens of the Two Rivers. And it was August, the heat was the cauldron that Iraqis still experience and the first creatures wanted to die. And God made it impossible for them. And some of us, descendants of these creatures, are in Paris, today, thinking this is our first journey and that an infinite one is waiting. An infinity of Paradise or one of Hell. It all looks so similar, we can't do much about it so why go on living with such an impotence? There are times when one feels that some things are more dreadful than death; it has to be life. It could be. I'll wear my coat and go out in the cold. The cold is not a problem, the air is. Should anyone fill his lungs with all this black stuff that hangs around, just to look at shops painfully similar in their desire to make us believe that they're indispensable? Walking in that bustle, and the difficulty, something else inhabits me, the knowledge that in the massive Church of Saint-Sulpice legions of angels reside, some visible, some not. I go there, often, regularly, and plunge into Delacroix's secretive world. The itinerary he followed from Place de Furstenberg to the church, the last years of his life, had been mine too when I lived on Rue Jacob under some linden trees. You enter the Chapel of the Holy Angels. It's an obscure place, very obscure, and your steps are uncertain. An angel is mounting a horse, a grey one, you're in a temple, the horse is trampling a handsome warrior, with its hoof is smashing his breast, while two other angels zero in on the fatal wound. The three draw a circle, a dance, the mounting angel has a halo, has wings, he is Saint-Michael the Archangel, Delacroix's messenger on earth. My eyes get used to the lit obscurity. I stare at the facing mural.

54

Jacob is still wrestling with his Angel. I'm at the bottom of the painting, then I'm in a forest, a valley, it could be Yosemite which in Delacroix's days was barely known to Europe, it has oak trees. Spiritual fights are secret and Jacob's men are running away, terrified, knowing that the battle is not carried on at the ordinary level of things. Jacob and the Angel are also embraced in a dance, their bodies glued in the confrontation of the Will against Love. Only in childhood do we have such a capacity to unify the world into a single image. The hues are green, the painted mural generates some light, oblique, the sky, below the trees, is reddening, the trees are taking sides: Nature and man can together prevail. They have been at it for so long. Shouldn't they take a rest? I'm home, and the fig tree in my courtyard is having a litter of premature little buds! Hallelujah! Who needs Easter after that? The electric lights are winning over the remains of "natural light." It will be a cold and long night. It will rain and the clothes in the bathroom won't dry. Water repels water, it seems. That's a political law that a socialist government would benefit by knowing. But this particular one is a pitiful racket. It will disappear into oblivion, like little crumbs in a sink. I'll light the gas in the kitchen, make myself a dinner. Once in the kitchen, I'll find out if there's something to eat, and look in the courtyard at the windows where no one ever seems to stand and look back. Instead of cooking a dinner I decided to go to the movies. I'm worried about not doing much these days: I dread these cinemas where you go underground for many floors. They're really catacombs. We submit ourselves to anything in a city like this. It's do or die. So I went to the Cosmos because at least it's large and at ground level. Ironically, it's also usually empty. They show exclusively Russian movies and, of course, they're in the wrong quarter. I saw *Lenin in France* by Youskevitch. Was it Youskevitch or Rohm? Should go back and check. Liked the film very much, but my pleasure was spoiled by the actor who played Lenin. Figures of History whose photographs and statues have been seen thousands of times cannot be played by actors. It's painful to see O'Toole play Lawrence of Arabia and some ham pretend he's Julius Caesar, another one make believe he's Van Gogh. These guys should be off the screens, like ghosts; yes, they're ghosts anyway. So, in fact, it's Paris that I liked in the film, not Lenin. I saw Montmarte, and Longjumeau, with their streets similar to those outside the movie house; the beautiful unity of French architecture in its billions of variations blew my mind. Windows are such miracles of craftsmanship, doors are so regal, or so proud, in their modesty or splendor, and the façades in between are sheets of music with all these visual notes. All through the film I have been amazed by the beauty of this fabulous human construction that this metropolis represents, expanded in time, space, peoples' minds, History, in dreams, in failures and triumphs, in being as well as in non-existence, all its colors framed on the scale which goes from black to white, a modulation which uses all the possibilities of the possible.

There is no use living in Paris when all one cares for is
the sea. Still, this is what thousands of people do, and what
I do, too. All around me, I see obstruction. I go into
churches not to pray but to get away from traffic and agita-
tion. Worshippers and tourists mingle while candles are
burning. I get some peace of mind by sitting in there, idly. I
must be searching for a religion, one which could tell me: it
happens that you are, and it will happen that you won't be.
In fact, this is what Paris says to everyone. It tells you to
be, the most you can, to be, and in the same time tells that
it won't matter that you won't be. I like hearing that song.
It's a clear political thing. "Conservatives" always tell you
that things will get better, if you only wait, standing behind them; churches whisper in your ear that if everything
failed, paradise would be earned by not complaining . . .
and there was Lenin who told them to work, paradise waiting at the end of many seasons. Those who sell illusions
win over those whose promises can be checked out. Political thinking can always be simplified. You can love the sea
and choose to live away from her. Things get tough, com-
plicated. Could I deny that Paris is no solid ground? Paris is
a sea and I'm one of its waves; look: the Seine is swelling
and pouring into the streets, and we are swimming. We are
the sea, and we ebb and flow with no itinerary. Here we
go, becoming a tempest, throwing Europe into a maël-

strom. We say yes, and we say no, we who are the center of eternal subversion. Who are these dark shapes running down the Avenues, hurrying towards multilayered shopping centers which are an immense failure although they shake the world? Is this somber basin resting on lime, crossed by a sinuous river, the parameter of the world? Why is this magnet attracting all political exiles who always think, despite all experience, that they'll find a freedom and security in this most dangerous of all places?! So much hope has lived and died at these walls' feet. We are in the greatest market for illusions that mankind has known. Behind these lit windows, up the stairs, the floors, within courtyards, there are conspirators, with their energy, women, men, from every possible country and those who dream that their country will exist one day. The latter plant their flags in their living-rooms. They live through expectation, conversation and the mail. They devour the same piece of news in ten different dailies, here they are, each in his favorite café, the one the police have carefully combed, and they think that they matter! They do, in a way. They are the signs of life that I try to detect in this cold, in this desolation. They cheer me more than pigeons will ever do. When I close my eyes, they enter my room, stay a while, with me, then leave. I never encounter them in a nightmare, which must be telling. I'm going to the Flore— again—I know the kind of raincoats I will see there, smelling of rubber, brand new, aseptic, little symbols of wealthy death. Working class cafés have closed around here. Europe doesn't work much, not in this part of town. A lot of immigrants work in factories and create a major problem: how to make them work without having them breathe our air, live in our cities, or look at our wives and husbands? This equation has not been solved. They go on with their menial jobs, genuinely happy to make a living. They love rain, asphalt, warm bread, goat cheese, industrial oils, long grocery hours. They see work as energy and life. People think it's incongruous that they smile in traffic jams. Paris is the machine that eats them and could reject them. What would you say if you became spit? You wouldn't know it. Spit doesn't think; it evaporates pretty fast. I'm not going to spit carelessly anymore. Out of respect for the street.

PARIS, WHEN IT'S NAKED

Of course, Paris is open to the round earth. It captures the planet's news, but what's shown on T.V. and printed in the papers isn't worthy of trust. Manipulation of information is the most perfected science of this century's end. It's not a matter of telling lies, and sometimes the cleverest form of disinformation is the telling of the truth. But there are ways of getting around it. Huge areas of the news are never touched. Others are closely selected, divided into bits, with missing parts, incompletion being a shrewd device. Information and propaganda have become so entangled that those who specialize in them acquire severe reality problems. The wheel keeps turning. People from the Third World are better at seeing through this fog; for them it's a matter of survival. Citizens from dominant countries fool themselves by thinking that they don't need to know: that's the beginning of the beginning of their downfall. As for me, most of what I want to know is not "news," not really. I want to see a whale in the ocean and be told how one can travel to the middle of the Indian Ocean, exactly when, for how much, and how to be sure to be able to come near the animal, or swim alongside his body. Whales are red-blooded and I would love to see them lose their temper, be jealous, contemplate the stars. I also would want to find out the whereabouts of the young English soldier I loved, in Beirut, during the Second World War. Newspapers are of no help in such cases. I forgot the name of his village in Yorkshire, but remember his name, and that could help. I won't dare, though, he may have died, since, and I'd sooner remember him alive. And beautiful. Paris is so huge, so full of people, that my thoughts get entangled in its electric wires and never reach their destination. Its tall buildings, aligned with no space between them save the streets, create an invincible screen to our feelings and dreams. You cannot fly in this city, you have to negotiate every move with it. This is why my thoughts keep close to the ground, picking up the soil's colors, meandering at low altitudes, always horizontally. That's not always as despairing as it sounds. By keeping such a low profile my thoughts can travel far, they can reach Poland, or, with a little push of the imagination, reach Moscow. My friend Pauline is there, and it helps. Russia! A brand new country, we're witnessing the birth of this new European baby, and my thoughts, in Moscow, can visit Pauline's. She's reading in libraries letters sent by some of Napoleon's soldiers in 1812. The Year of the Great Cold. In the coldest winter of our own century she's reading about ice, death by freezing, empires being done and undone by a commander who was always there and to whom nobody ever gave an army: the Field-Marshal Winter of all the Russias. My poor thoughts got scared and retreated, running. I shall store them in a warm place. Oh! a knock at my door. I have to open. It's Monsieur Bacchus, my wine merchant who delivers my bottles of Volvic. I told him I'm switching to Vittel but he prefers Volvic and won't deliver the other. I let him do as he pleases. At least, he lets me choose the wines. It's late in the stairway, dark. The bottles are in. I feel better. I can go out for a little walk, see if they changed the bookstore's windows. What an ugly corner! My favorite books are already read. Paris is a good place for books, not that it reads them all, but there are plenty. One book per inhabitant. I keep going back to my favorite poet, as I said, Hölderlin. Paris becomes Hölderlin, who followed every cloud. He would have been puzzled by this city where one can see no cloud in its entirety. He would have loved it, because of his big heart. But I remember that one day he cried, and wrote these lines:

> You cities of the Euphrates!
> and you, streets of Palmyra!
> you forests of pillars on the desert's face,
> what became of you!

The Orient's phosphorescence is unbearable for the countries of the West . . . I can see Hölderlin in Paris, with his forgiveness, his infinite comprehension. The sacred fire has disappeared. So Paris will do. They understand ashes, here. Our incinerated hearts find a receptacle in this circular city whose own heart is a bridge, isn't it? I can always trust a city with bridges, regardless of the pain. There is something resembling hope, in suspension. A thrust over a void. A life stream against death. And reflections! Can we live without arches and reflections? no! it would be living without water, and that's impossible. When things get unbearable, there remain the banks of the Seine. Noisy, I know it too well, taken over by the city's weight. Still, they are there, for the mind, if not for the body, with, sometimes, many patches of light.

It's the early hours of the day that are the most memorable in Paris. It was during the war in Beirut, one of its worst moments, Tell Zaatar was under siege, and I was unable to sleep. So with the break of dawn I used to leave my studio on Rue Paul-Louis Courier and take the Boulevard going East. Boulevard Saint-Germain in these early hours is a majestic artery of the city. It was built with imagination when the French had a sense of grandeur, an inflated one at times, but a real one. They sensed that their citizens needed room around their shoulders when they walked, and a large horizon. The boulevard, in these hours, is an epic road. Trees, on each side, breathe easily, their leaves quivering with the breeze. They make a canopy for glory. In this magnificence I was walking in the middle of the boulevard like someone making a triumphal march. And in the secret of my heart I was broken with defeat. Tell Zaatar was the signal for further disaster. The Flore was still closed, its chairs piled up neatly within its glass doors. Very few people were out and the city could belong to us, the few. As soon as the Church of Saint-Germain was open, I would go in, day after day, just sitting in its coolness, and thinking: Oh God! if you exist, help them there. But in utter tragedy there are moments of great happiness. On my way back, with traffic starting to roll, I used to enter the Flore, be its first customer, have the café all to myself, its mirrors reflecting its bottles, sink in its half awake morning light, and make a café au lait and a croissant stretch as long as possible. Thus some of the hardest times my mind has ever gone through were also those where Paris was given back to me, for my secret enchantment. Later in the day, things used to change. Something terrible was always at hand. Other cities and their terror merged with this one. Ambulances were blowing their sirens, homes were being broken into, the key to my door didn't work, some telephone lines hung loose, should I call the police or the locksmith? People are getting used to break-ins; to accept anything. Oh! it started with benign things: the noise? why not? Prices are going up, but doesn't that mean prosperity? Too many malfunction cases in the hospitals, but doctors are human. Government officials are corrupt and who isn't? Newspapers are biased, so are their readers. Liberties are being chewed at but you can always choose from one of many restaurants. Africa is in chronic strife, so we keep the Foreign Legion there, where adventure lies. So one day the police can fill its vans and we'll shake our shoulders and read some obscure treatise on Heidegger's merits. Unless it be Wittgenstein. We're not going to put Western civilization on trial because some wretched immigrant has been deported. Look at his own country, is it any better? I don't need, like tourists do, to go to special quarters and search for some reality different from mine. There are clochards in any arrondissement, medieval buildings in any street (almost), French wines in any market. You can dance anywhere, if you have the right address. You can (it doesn't happen often) be murdered in front of the mairie. You end up being satisfied to stay close to your home. I'm a passenger, in this city, itself a little planet on planet Earth. Every other person is in my situation. Look, the Tunisian grocer is closing his store and going home, wearing a threadbare coat although he must have a lot of money in his bank account. There, an African from Senegal is hurrying to the metro. He's used to the cold but not to the loneliness this cold creates in his bones. Below, there is a restaurant with Indian food. No saris enter, only young Parisians who love spices. I know that European stores will soon follow. We were dreaming in the dear old 60's of a life with fewer objects around. Now matter is eating us raw. Space is stifled by cars, traffic, buses, lorries, people . . . and inside, it's worse, much worse. In the houses traffic moves with even more difficulty, I mean bodies, air-currents, guests . . . Everything has come to a stop. These elegant Paris apartments are full of boxes within boxes. In fact, they're asphyxiating. Don't try to come in.

PARIS, WHEN IT'S NAKED

On Sunday afternoons Paris's avenues seem to be dilated, as if the houses were there only to trace the frontiers of these enormous corridors. These canyons can be envied by the valleys of the Americas. There's an enchantment to such open sky labyrinths, avenues made for the soul to expand and meander within its own thoughts and desires. One's breathing expands, too. There's a majestic silence to this place so clearly *built*, stone on stone, space on space, a delirious freedom for the body between landmarks left by centuries, a corner, a 17th century habitation, its stone polished to become silk, so many human adventures having taken place under its windows. A sentiment of solitary conquest accompanies you in your walks. In this quincentennial of Columbus's "discovery" I can't help thinking of the American continent's bloody epics. My favorite figure is Bolivar. I hear him say to his woman: "You will be alone, Manuela. And I will be alone, in the middle of the world. There will be no more consolation than the glory of having conquered ourselves." There's great recognition of loneliness in the people that I see, as if loneliness were the only way to greatness left to us. But what is this *self* that Bolivar conquered? The self is mercury, my favorite metal, it breaks to pieces when you come too close. It practically doesn't exist. This is why I feel alright when it's hazy outside, in mist, in fog, because that's what we are, little clouds that any wind can shatter. And then, there's Lenin. His Revolution washed out, like Spain's imperial designs. At last, one can start thinking about him, freely. He belongs to History which means that he's harmless. For the better, and for the worst. What about his dream? his utopia? What about the peoples of the world? Paris is too wealthy a place for one to ask such questions. It is a fairground for illusions. But the walls can come down, Pandora's box can spill its ills and fill the air. We don't know what's coming, which is wonderful, really. Not knowing is richer in possibilities than knowing. There's turmoil in the air, change. I love this gaping space in front of me, this sky which is not of today's. Of course, it turns too suddenly into a tunnel, and here I stand, rejected into a night, and why not, this night looks like a movie-house before the projection. When the sky is low, memories fly low too, and eyes move swiftly on the surface of things. My heart beats fast. I will sit and wait, forget the lakes which continue to expect rain on their high plateaux. A nightmare may appear anytime, with its sounds, while I'm comfortably seated. It takes comfort and good health to be miserable. We know these things, as we know that the sky is a convenient canopy. Behind the hypocrisy lie the memories of bliss, and the rose-colored deserts that many abandon in favor of the mind's aridity. I am not here, today, I am in a distant paradise, the valley of Yosemite, walking on clean granite, in the fifth season of the year, receiving on my face the waterfalls's spindrift. Yes, there are days when, in Paris, I'm totally elsewhere. This city has the power to propel you out of it, vigorously, and I can't fight that ultimate power which makes me feel not only not here, but not existing at all.

This old desire for ritual which leads all the way to execution and cannibalism, expresses itself, given the accumulation of laws, and the fear of facing sacred terror, in political fights. Anything is blown into a "scandal," any unexpected move by the party in power becomes a pretext seized by the opposition for lashing out with violent invectives. This process gives birth to an accumulation of mythologies which could be very explosive. Can we, for ever, as a species, control our destiny, or are we to disappear in sheer irrationality? An avalanche of doubts besets me while I walk on the city's messy sidewalks. Would this greyness, periodically visited by the sky's intrusion, last forever? Would generations, after my passage, enjoy the bitterness I feel, this sign of the importance we attribute to our selves? Otherwise I would have had the lightness I witness in foxes when they run and jump over fences . . . Tourists sit in the cold in the few cafés which set their tables in open air, and not being different from pigeons, they come to where there's food and water, regardless of the weather. Those who are not in the streets are in their hotel rooms facing their T.V. set. Opium in China, hashish in Egypt, used to keep populations in a state of somnolence. Nowadays our political systems keep us hypnotized by flickering images. Where's the change? The difference? The lone bird which invariably draws a straight line with its flying body has no answers. And why is Lenin leaning so heavily on my mind? Because of an empire's undoing, recently, a huge cardboard castle's thunder of continental proportions? There is always the incredible failure of an incredible dream. Millions of workers were going to be masters of History. They were going to *know* it . . . The question of what would have happened had Lenin lived longer is a useless one. The new question is *Russia.* With no question mark. As for Paris, no revolutionary fever is animating it. A feeling of sameness pervades the city. The poor forget they're human and become objects to which you do or don't give a franc. Under the habitual misery a new level is being reached, and it doesn't stir anger, pity, or guilt. It happens, though, that sometimes some of those under-bums take revenge, not on you, or me, but on something invisible that their minds comprehend supremely: call it life, call it God. They squat on the Odeon Theatre's stairs, and when the shows are over and the doors closed, when it's freezing, deep in the night, with few pedestrians happening to cross the Place, they put on their own act, recite their seemingly incoherent verses, improvise complete plays, and collapse on the cold stone without stirring a leaf. How can I witness such a scene with pleasure, which in fact I do?! In the bottom of the selfishness which is the core of any being, a communion with a moment of truth brings real happiness. Paris is a working proposition, with corners of utmost elegance; it functions better than any other metropolis, this awesome machinery has the sublime property of not crushing too many of its inhabitants. We're not in hell's deepest layers, we're out of the paradise-purgatory-hell trinity. We're part of the new collective and creative energy growing steadily and chewing up frontiers. Would Paris and Berlin connect one day, uninterruptedly? I have to deal with familiar obsessions. European unity is starting with euphoria. Europeans are giving it a chance; they project a millenium of prosperity. In fact they want to pick up the pieces left by Charlemagne's death. What is time? Something constantly reduced to nothingness. Where is Charlemagne? He could have died a few minutes ago. His state of non-being would have been the same. The tides which moved ahead since his disappearance receded to their point of departure. From Paris to Moscow there's a railroad, an air route, and a ride. Paris never ceased to believe that Russians have a soul while Russians came to doubt it. Is that soul going to elevate us again, as Nijinsky did, we who do need elevation? Paris sinks a few inches a year (Venice too), I don't know where it's going. Where is anything going? Where this bus? This bird? This cloud? Where do we think we're going? Ideologies, for the time being, are shot down. I know that some of us think we're aiming at Paradise. Do we organize societies for an after-world? And what of those for whom Paradise never made sense? I have this tranquil belief that we're going nowhere, *there* is here, always here. I'm going to the kitchen, or to California. Strangely, it's the same. Trees don't go anywhere, and still, they do, they grow branches which move, leaves, which fall, they get fat, they wither, they even die. *They move.* I'm going to the Luxembourg. I miss it, miss the octogonal fountain. I grew to love, also, the Medici fountain. It's sunk deep, always in the shade, its waters feeling more wet than the others. Trees bend over it, keeping a conversation going. It's a cool place, like inside one's brain. I never stay around it for a long time because I love it, and do with it like I do with people. The more they matter to me the more I avoid them. It's an incapacity to live by my passions. They overwhelm me, the slightest sentiment does, always, always. I love the Medici fountain so I slow my pace, look at it, follow its undulating surface, swim (mentally) with its fish, come the closest I can to the essence of its shades of green which make my heart pound. Then I fly over it, carefully, like a butterfly, absorb its coolness while moving along its borders, and I become water, friend of water.

PARIS, WHEN IT'S NAKED

So we went in, and it was a place without music, and it was immediately noticeable that men were all dressed and women barely covered. There were small bars on that first floor, and we weren't seated yet when I sensed eyes directed towards us. It was darkish, trying to look intimate. The couples I saw were rather young, obviously provincial.

71

They must have thought that they had come to catch the city's essence, Paris, where you leave your feathers, shed your skin. It didn't take too long for my companion to get interested in a female body. He put on his best smile, said a few things in a low tone of voice, the young woman took his hand into hers. Fifteen minutes later he was all over her, a squirrel over a nut. The game which ruled this club required that I get involved with her partner, and that wasn't, for me, a foregone conclusion. I thought, let's go, he would do for preliminary talks. We went into a tiny room with pink wallpaper and soft lights. In these random encounters sexual desires are released in small doses. It's important to use a lot of time, to make the night last as long as possible, reminding one of the days (and nights) of real love. I lost track of my friend. Oh! he's grunting and moaning. Men become children in such moments, or at least it's what women like to think. Not their mothers, of course. If only they knew! My friend comes out of his cubicle. His cheeks are flushed. He's all buttoned up. He feels like paying, and leaving. My partner is still exercising patience; he tries to keep a conversation going, but I never knew how to say all the trivialities which make life smoother. I didn't really bargain for this exchange of transient "lovers." All I can tell is that the young man who's facing me is going to get bored, pretty soon, or angry. He lent his girl-friend and didn't get much in return. How did you find this place, I asked him. The way you did, he said. He saw me astonished by his answer, and became friendly again. And he said: I checked on the Minitel, the first one. Now we come often. And when I asked him if he was usually satisfied, he looked slightly, very slightly, upset, and he said: she gets to attract them more than I attract women. I looked him straight in the face. You're pretty handsome, I thought, you shouldn't worry. My head was spinning. I wanted to leave. His mistake was to have mentioned the word Minitel. I use the Minitel for the news (when I don't use it to call a taxi). This cave, or call it a cavern, meant for love making, is stifling. I'd rather get out. But I like my partner. I've sensed his vulnerable spot. He must have good relations with his colleagues, wherever he works. Must have gone to French schools, must have corrected his spelling on school-children's notebooks. I hesitated, then I asked him point blank: have you ever been in love? He refused to answer. He said: let's speak of something else, and I said of what? He said: of you. That was embarrassing. Me. Who was I in this dark lurid place, me whose curiosity (and boredom) led to such a non-interesting place, next to this young man, this nice fellow? Maybe I would have found many things to tell him about me, if only we were sitting together at the Café de la Mairie. The café was far, far away. But here? I asked for some wine. He pushed his own glass in front of me, then ordered a new glass for himself. The two glasses were sitting next to each other, like us, frozen. I wanted to be honest, tell him that there was a war, a "Desert Storm," start talking about the fires, the new Deluge of burning oil, of sand, of burning sand, of children, of dead children, and I started thinking my God!, if I were to tell him all this, in this darkness, with all these unfulfilled sexual desires floating around us, he might go crazy, he might get violent, and dangerous, or cry like a baby, like what women think he is. None of this happened. He let me know that he wasn't political at all. Politicians are corrupt, he said, we pay them to be so, he added. I work and I like fun, he continued. I come here to unwind. It's good for the soul. Beatrice and I may get married one day. We don't know. She's sitting there. She's through, you know. He looked at me carefully. I knew he couldn't see her; the door was closed. He said: serious people shouldn't come here, they spoil the game, and life is serious enough, out there. Here, let's drink. You make me thirsty. Let's be smart, I thought, unhappy about the dullness of the situation. His eyes lit. You know, he said, people don't need to have intercourse. Then he asked: do you know how frogs make love, and answered his own question: a female frog carries her male for as long as a month, he fecundates her eggs while they're dropping . . . I thought: there is matter for wonder in the non-human world, and maybe salvation.

Why am I living in Paris? Because I speak French? That could be a major reason, but it's not. If I had the choice, I would have loved to be Cavafy, living in Alexandria, in his times. But why Paris? Many reasons would keep me rather away from it. For one: the hospitals. Paris's hospitals could be sinister, and its doctors, crazy. Paris is also, I wish I could sometimes forget it, a colonial capital. The capital of a colonial empire. The coffees we drink, the rubber we roll on, the precious wood we buy . . . are suspicious products; we don't know if they're paid a fair price for . . . or extorted by "diplomatic" means. When does trade become moral, or immoral? Why do I love this somber city, give my life to its streets, spend it in its restaurants, break it under its melancholy—why? Should I get to know myself in order to know why Paris is so central to my life, or should I know this city even more than I do to find out at least a few essential things about myself? These questions could also be mere traps. But then, what should I do? Do what I have always done: keep going to the movies, bookstores, into alleys, parks, places which do attract me, Barbès, at night, Place des Vosges, at 10 in the morning, that perfect square which is fenced like the very idea of France, neatly defined. I love the oyster bars of Montparnasse because of the smell. I go there and think of Brittany, which I seldom visit. The ocean penetrates Paris in subversive ways, mostly through the treachery of fish markets: some salt, some iodine, and you have the Atlantic in your nostrils. There's also, there's always, this question of poetry that we can't dissociate from Paris. Great poets did happen elsewhere, and maybe the greatest ones, who were Chinese, Persians, or Arabs. I cannot read Hafiz by the banks of the Seine. He'll catch a fever, go straight home to bed. Paris is no rose garden and no Persian poetry will grow in it. It's hopeless. But there's a poet who hovers above the city, and that's Mallarmé. Yes, Paris is inseparable from the idea of poetry. That's a mirage, one cay say. But we live by mirages, there's no way to know a mirage from an oasis; after all, a reflection has the reality of being a reflection, can you say no to that? I drove through mirages and they came on each side of the car; no bother. I'll have to come back to Mallarmé, our friend. This 19th century poet is still ahead of us. Grand priest of poetry, his endeavor led him to Nothingness, that absolute opening, Greek chaos, matrix. But who's going to tell what the ultimate book will be in this City of Books? Did Mallarmé mean that his Book would be an ultimate Revelation? Is the Blank Page the last Revelation? In the meantime we slide gracefully towards images, ephemeral configurations which suit the new nomadic spirit of our times. This is the year of the Indian's return, in Latin America, and the end of "France," with Europe's birth: a cataclysmic year in greatest silence. It's a season of death and resurrection for the continent's nations. Rain is falling, shining on zinc roofs, blackening streets, moistening bones. I'm witnessing through various channels a white revolution. Russian peasants are taken by surprise. Messiahs have failed them so often that they hang on the world as they know it. I share their apprehensions, I'm accustomed to love things Russian: their women, their men, their icons, their music, their anarchy. Their anarchy above all. If I were sure to die in a few days I'd read one of their novels, and read Akhmatova, right here, in Paris, ideal city of readers. If you miss anybody, or anything, come to Paris, it's a good place for such a state of the soul. It will fill your heart's empty corners. It's not a romantic place, it's a place for romance. In its hotels you will find some of the worst mattresses you ever slept on, and peeled wall paper, but you will be received at their desk as if you were a gentleman on his off days, or the run-away wife of a Greek skipper. There's a quietness of the spirit in the cheapest hotels that calls for love affairs, and little tables in them on which one can write only love letters. Breakfast is a rendez-vous with the morning papers and the tourists' tired eyes. Sleepless nights are good in Paris: they're peopled with fantasies. Past and present mingle as in fairy tales. And to be alone doesn't mean dejection, but, rather, hope . . . You hear street noises and they become intimate confidences. You can't bear not being in love, while in Paris, and you don't know why. A secret fever accompanies you everywhere, like it used to when you were an adolescent, and maybe, secretly, you hope it stays that way because one comes here primarily to dream. For those who stay longer, experiences become non-erasable memories, because this stage for happiness cannot be replaced. It's also a wonderful place to be unhappy in, forgetting the rented rooms and the ecstasy they sheltered, for Paris stirs sadness without dragging you to desperation. I wouldn't commit suicide in it, no, if it came to that there would be many things I would still like to do that would act as music does: I would look at the river, its beauty would refuse to accommodate my body; I would go to the Fontaine des Innocents, and memory would bring my steps back to the Luxembourg (let's hope this happens in late autumn so that the Garden's incredible beauty will lend structure to my over-spilling thoughts). This is a city built by Desire for people who never understood their real self, and now these will cease to be what they have been for a few millenia in order to become European, wearing new shoes that will take them no one knows where, if not to a new and implosive imperial design.

PARIS, WHEN IT'S NAKED

The light is dirty. Objects gather energy, and even chairs, today, look half-human. We have so much intimacy with them that I'm surprised they don't start learning foreign languages. But when the light is inimical, it becomes very difficult to move. Some sort of blockage takes place, the kind of feeling you get when you run into sandbags. There must be something I can do in the house: start a book. I can't find something I want to read on the bookshelves that surround me. I dust off a table, then start worrying about all those minutes I lose, a loss which brings me closer to the hour of my death. How and when would I die? You would think a sleepwalker is asking this question. I put aside such morbid thoughts and go to the kitchen. Nothing to eat, there, that tastes really good. Have you ever taken time to eat a yoghurt. Eat, or drink, one. I don't know what you do with it. There are vegetables, too, but they remind me of pesticides. Paris is dark and heavy today. You can't shake its walls. I love its curving roads which all look straight until you come full circle. Each shop is a life's story. Each building is Balzac, all over again. So much money moves from hand to hand. Merchandise slides over counters and beer, good beer, is distributed—but not for free—for the asking. Don't go to the Closerie des Lilas anymore, stay at the Flore. It doesn't matter if it's full of smoke, and also full of people, and noisy to a painful degree. You're sitting with ghosts, there, friendly ones. As soon as you arrive, at any moment of the day, or the night, something tells you that Picasso and Sartre just left. My friend René left too. He was their favorite waiter. One day I asked him what he did for his summer. He answered: "J'ai fait du cinéma!", then explained carefully that he has a super-8 and proudly added that he had filmed the Police charging, in May 68! I should call him and see his films. I have now to cross to the Church, then turn left. The light is full of particles, the ones nobody studies but that we all breathe, or, I must say, eat. The eating capital of the world serves you great Bordeaux with marinated gigots, and then you spit black things, with resignation. Since Roman times the Seine flows to your left, when you come down Rue Bonaparte. Aren't you better off at home, waiting for phone calls? And all these foreigners, how quickly they become French: friendly, distant, busy, impervious to your loneliness, theirs being greater. You have to be heroic to live in Paris. And why such emphasis on food, in this city? There's great food, of course, and restaurants which are fun: they are live stories, picture-book places, folk-art in themselves. In the night, they shine like magic-lanterns. They have also something else. Food is there to be eaten: you cannot manipulate it ad infinitum. And the only person I trust, really, is my stomach. It doesn't lie, rejecting anything spoiled, giving everything it absorbs its due, and is seldom betrayed, in this city. I can't say that much about the mayor of the VIème arrondissement or the President of the country. This is why it is heroic to lead such non-heroic lives. The pain is tremendous. All these non-entities! where would I show myself and be welcome, when will they know that I intend neither to buy nor to praise? Looking at the pavement, my coat usually buttoned up, I go as if I mattered, read the paper with a prime-minister's intensity, read books thinking I belong to the club; I look at pictures with a professional's eye; something tells me it's all a game, a loser's one. If I died, here, and now, one person, for sure, would cry, another one would be sorry, and that's about all, and that's true of every one who is an exile, and the human race is in exile. Maybe ants carry long funerals and mourn for many seasons. Human ants have lost the key to ritual suffering. They disintegrate, that's all. There's ink on my table, and some paper. I could write a few letters and re-establish lines with far away friends. The metaphors don't come easily, these days, and my letters to them do not tell who I am. I copy their own style, I presume. They never tell me that their sleep is interrupted by my absence. So, what's left to say? Very little. They promise a party for my return, and one, I suppose, for my new departure. In between, we'll all be too busy. And long stretches of asphalt will keep us apart. Let's not nourish fantasies about friendship. It's an ingredient in our lives which is sold-out. New stocks aren't coming. Since the downfall of their empire, the Russians don't produce any, either. They liberalized their prices, tomatoes are scarce, their tears, even more so. Nobody dances in Saint Petersburg. The old ballerina-masters had left with the Czar, through Asia. The new ones are leaving on airplanes. No friends, no tomatoes. What's freedom's use? Don't ask Voice of America. That voice has been shut up, its people out of a job, victims of their success. It's good to be in Paris, where Liberty made sense, at least for a while, and where the cold is less severe than in Croatia. Good. I'll go to Place Clichy and look at the bars. There's solid life there. Sexual appetite thrives on the Right Bank. The other appetite is left for this bank, the intellectual one, the one with all those people who think that Greek Thought is for the birds. There's a new order in the world, a new thought done by electronic devices. It beats the Greeks at every corner and is not prone to suicide. No hemlock for the Macintosh. These patriotic machines will do the job for us, while we attend to our daily chores. They leave the dusting and the ironing to us. And when work at home gets stifling, you can always go out your door, take the elevator, say hello to the concierge, press a button, exit, and once in the street, pouf! it rains, a bit, a soft rain, some space, trees in the distance, your hand, in your pocket, holding your keys, and you go two, three blocks, ahead, two, or three, right, you close the circle and are back home, your home.

PARIS, WHEN IT'S NAKED

Today, should I say again that it's a day similar to all the others, I go into the street knowing already the outcome of my effort. No meadow is within reach, no angel is waiting, no promise has been made that this moment will burst. Too predictable a city, too many obstacles for any horse to gallop freely. I slow down my pace, which is not fast, by any means, but something slackens within me too, and drags my feet into the eternal Café de la Mairie du VIème, which is standing there, its neon lights turned on, its waiters constantly in a hurry. I'm sitting with my newspaper spread on the table. An Algerian poet stands at the bar's corner, sometimes with a small glass of beer, sometimes with a big one. Malek continuously scribbles on tiny pieces of paper and I don't think that all the lines to which he gives birth are poems. Once in a while I stop by him, say hello, ask how he feels, and he invariably tells me he's all right, Algeria is all right, the world is all right. I believe none of it. But Paris has its ways and manners, it conditions people not to be too personal. They write it down, when they want to. The talking is done at the psychoanalyst. "Educated" people never say interesting things. When I reach a point of suffocation with so much emptiness, I eavesdrop on my neighbors' conversations, in cheap restaurants, and I'm blessed with all kinds of accents and topics. Last night, the topic was Algeria, the War of Independence, and torture. One woman was claiming that the French Army had its torture chambers. After much debate the one next to her said that after all nobody was mentioning that the Arabs used torture too, in that same war. And that seemed fair enough, to say such a thing, and I was almost happy to hear it, when the man who was dining with the two women said: "But we're not Arabs, we're civilized people, and we shouldn't have done such terrible things!" I started feeling bad about something I couldn't define, my food tasted poorly, I didn't like this new Italian place on Rue Racine, and I was ready to go home the shortest way possible. The night was fine, it had stopped raining, the sky seemed to be as it was centuries ago, and the road had to be longer, so I went up Boulevard Saint-Michel, felt homesick for the Orient, the one nobody can define, reached the Luxembourg's south border, stuck my nose through its fence, and, of course, came home. It was starting to rain and I felt happy in my armchair watching winter games on T.V. On the little screen huge mountains were rising and beautiful young women were mightily descending the most dangerous slopes. Such a wonderful scene. Leopards and gazelles give less thrill than the human body speeding down on skis! Men followed, German, Austrian, Japanese . . . carried by the desire to conquer, with no other weapons than their own bodies, with no enemy other than fear, no battlefield other than mountains and snow. I went far away into the possibilities of a body I didn't have. It's true that I dread great storms, the spiritual ones above all. My attention stretched to its limits. The champions have been skiing under an intense snow fall. I looked at a screen covered with white-in-motion, as if it became an electron microscope. It drew me into it, my tired mind spinning and going sideways, which I had to keep pulling back into what became a moving nothingness. But nothingness and I are long-time friends, and it was one of the most meaningful hours of my life. The snow continued to come in diagonals, and between the diagonals were other lines made of snow, falling, modulating the air as they were modulating my vision. Between all these diagonal lines I was able to perceive shadows, white shadows, so to speak, separating the falling threads. A new fatigue chased away the old one, I was left alone with the feeling of being here, there, and in front of me was the intense experience of a space leading to the muscular sensation of moving forward without a displacement of any sort. Is Paris a question of the particular quality of its space? Would that inner space, I mean the spacey image of its "real" space, shrink with Paris's importance in the world to come? Those who will live here, in this house, by this window, and will call it Europe, will they feel crammed in or will they experience a dilation of their spirit to their wish's dimensions? Paris is a circle, infinite and circumscribed, a mandala. Although nothing Eastern makes sense to it, it attracts the East like a magnet. Iranians and Hindus see it as one of their initiation's best stations. They can cheat with it without cheating, knowing the nature of its attractiveness: a mixture of greyness with a breeze, of rigidity with a river, of low skies with tall trees, of common sense with folly, of knowledge with unfathomable ignorance. All of this mixed with an ingredient that nobody knows and that everybody senses. Paris can be nowhere, when you close your eyes, when you write a letter, can be all forgotten, but suddenly it surges from under your feet, and you're dazzled by its black brilliance. Then you can advance, or stay still, your movements won't matter anymore. You may die soon after and you won't know it. Your insecurity could drag you to genuine madness and hospitals, but it will come later. You are seeing green and red lights simultaneously, you're floating, walking and standing still, you're dizzy and lucid about it, and lucid without it, you're here, and across yourself, and out of yourself, and you're pure being at the most concentrated degree possible, to the point of infinity.

PARIS, WHEN IT'S NAKED

Paris is a place for encounters. Everything converges to it and that's why its cafés hold such magic: the world comes to them while you're sitting, human life meets its destiny. I was at the Saint-Claude, idle, daydreaming. The table next to mine was vacant. A man came to sit. I noticed that he was fat. There was something timid, clumsy, about him. I turned my gaze away, but my thoughts were not reaching far, and I turned again his way. Our eyes met. Something stirred deep within me. My blood started to run faster. His clothes were no clue. He smiled, and his smile unveiled him: he was the young man I had met in the deepest fog I have ever experienced. I think I pronounced his name, softly, I said: Henri, and he said he was wondering if he was right in recognizing me. At least thirty-five years had gone by since I last saw his smile. I couldn't remember when and where. We had met by chance, in the total invisibility of a fog, and we were again sitting next to each other, with words rushing to our throats. Why did he start by telling me: I'm free. And you? He was to go to Poitiers, he told me, the last day we had met, to the university of his home town. He became a lawyer, he now said, and got married. I asked if he had any children, the answer was no. He asked me what happened to me, since, and I told him it was too long a story to tell. We were talking a bit, and remaining silent . . . He was ordering some draft beer, and cold air was coming in with each new customer. What happened to your friend Bunny, he asked, and I said that she committed suicide, many, many years ago. You loved Paris so much, then, he remembered. I still do, I said. I felt close to him, friendly. The time-machine was transforming its ways. I noticed that he still wore a tweed jacket, that his eye-glasses had pale rims. He told me he was teaching a course at the Faculty of Law. Poitiers is quieter than Paris, he said. Then he blushed, and added, but you never loved me, why? He was becoming Orpheus and going into a labyrinth searching for what had happened. His beer was shining in its glass, the foam quieting down. Then he said: excuse me, it wasn't that dramatic, I have a good life. I remembered how, as a young man, he was obsessed with sexual matters, at least at a conversational level. It used to strike me as funny. I was at the opposite end, I couldn't talk about it. I was happy to have him in front of me, seeing that he had kept his basic integrity, a touch of melancholy, something very candid. Henri was mysterious by being very honest with himself, in a clumsy, indirect, almost twisted way. His curiosity was boyish (his forehead, too). I tried to find the thread that would lead me to the past; he was, I had a feeling, trying to catch up with the moment we were living. We talked of Paris, the place being the crucible of our identities. Who were we? If we could recapture this, we would understand why we didn't love each other with the madness we expected. We started evoking the streets we walked then. We recalled our hours at the Café de Tournon, and he was getting slimmer, his eyes were getting clear, and I was sitting in front of him as a young woman feeling that the city was built for my own sake and that this young Frenchman was meant to be my escort, my shadow in the streets that we were walking, making of these walks a subtle erotic exercise. Then Henri said that he seldom came to Paris, Poitiers had become his life, and that he usually visited it to buy books. He didn't know I had gone to America, and he only said: why? Then asked for how long I was in France but the answer didn't seem to matter to him. I asked him, to break the silence, if he was happy with his marriage. He said oh yes! and then got embarrassed, and told me that he was basically impotent, oh! not in my heart! he hurried to add, but you know, he said, it never worked, and when she has affairs on her own I almost feel happy, she's very nice, you know. Things started to fall into their proper place. We were coming close to the tunnel's end, nearing the light. Henri was a man who had stayed in my memory. A strange affection linked me strongly to him. I could have played in kindergarten or run under pine forests with him at age eleven. He became totally familiar to me the very moment I barely guessed his features in that thick fog, where it didn't matter if it was night or day, the single moment maybe when I loved him. I was now approaching him, perceiving the light, in this obscure afternoon. People were moving outside, going to myriads of activities. I saw his face get pale, his smile calling Time to his rescue. Things became clear because I had never before bothered to look back on our situation. Henri had come one night at the Cité Universitaire's American Pavilion, where I was living, with an older man. He introduced him as a Canadian philosopher. We went to dinner somewhere in the Xème arrondissement, I remember. We walked in the night a long time, his friend talked a lot. He was telling me that he had been a priest, a well-known Jesuit theologian, and that he had been expelled from his Order. Henri admired him for a double reason: he felt at home with a man who had been immersed in catholicism, like his own parents, and who had been rebellious against something they both knew intimately. Our Canadian friend wanted to go to Rue de Lappe. Movies, novels, were then turning the street into a legend. He wanted to go dancing. Henri was in awe. I sensed this man's power over Henri's mind. He had come between us, like Doctor Faust, whom I had just read of and taken seriously, and I was terrified by Faust (and by Western Civilization), and the evening mixed everything into an atmosphere of excitement and strangeness. Henri was being chivalrous, not so much with me as with the ex-priest, he was literally pushing me into complicity with this ominous character. I tried to remind Henri of the evening. He seemed to have no recollection. He only said that he lost track of his friend when he went back to Poitiers. That was all. But I understood, at last, what had happened; it was very simple. The Canadian danced with me, and he was getting amorous, then we sat for a while, and he was practically on his knees begging me to become his, then we danced and he started talking into my ear his obsessions, his affairs with the young boys of his seminary, and he was saying that he was looking for the perfect being who would fulfill his basic bisexuality, that he was desperate, that he had found me. His desperation was real, was tragic. An ageing man was begging his life from me, right there, in public, impervious to the music, the hour, the people. I felt a strong repulsion, as cruel as that must have been. I was possessed by the city. I only saw the priesthood, the insistence. Too many complexities were thrown at me all at once. I felt sacred terror. And Henri was associated with the whole thing, and I saw an old man collapse, surrounded by music and conversations, and when Henri found a young doctor in the room, they took the man to his hotel. Afterwards I lost interest in Henri. Now I'm telling Henri that I live nearby, Rue Madame. He smiles. (I remember that he had compassion for everything, and that I had compassion for him.) It's very close to the Law school that I was going to when we knew each other, he says. I love the Quartier. So you live nearby? I wish I could, too. Who would have said we'd meet again. What do you drink, coffee? Have a beer, he says.

PARIS, WHEN IT'S NAKED

Why? In spite of geometric stillness, and that sheet of old silver which fills upper space, reluctantly, knowing the sacrilege, two pigeons move slightly on the small building's roof which barely reaches my windowsill's level. They move and manage to look not alive. What can we do? Wait for spring, even if a tentative one, to arrive into this enclosed courtyard whose huge walls stand erect but are not impressive? Is my inkpot tired of feeding my thoughts? Would all these pencils, instead of staring at me, start a revolution in their own world, and, maybe, leave? They probably do all these things during my sleep. How can we know what things do when we're not watching? There is this ache which moves around my heart; it's not asking for help. Big rains, big rains, where are you? To be here, without you, knowing you went to California, is to be an orphan. The storms happen over landscapes that I know, in my own familiar lands, while I'm waiting within Paris's heart, for some minute consolation. Where did the illuminations go? Should we for ever be in *transition*, transitional transitions, not having known the beginning, big bang or whisper, and doomed to not see the end? In the meantime we have to make some good of the few streets we love, something worth the imagination granted to us by Nature, and make of a street as narrow as Rue Férou, or the Rue Servandoni, something worth the fact that we have been born. What a singular thing, a birth, a visit to Earth, a participation in the latter's glory, and misery! How would I manage to comprehend such a City within my tired head?! A whiff of fresh air, a breeze, the night's fall on stone buildings, and the immense wound of the Garden, the model for all Gardens, now that the Garden of Eden has been so thoroughly destroyed by the American bombers: suddenly all this comes together and there's a tiny explosion of truth, a second, a fraction of a second of some miraculous bit of meaning which touches gently my brain. Then all disappears. Paris becomes a place, a location with which I can't measure myself, not an alien, no, never, but some beast that consumes me, as well as others, and remains equal to itself. This is when I go back to Charlemagne, try to start at point zero. Mind you, I don't identify with French History, not at all. I use it as an ideal yard-stick, the one I learned before anything else. So I go back to Charlemagne, Europe's Father image, and from there I can fly over nations at war, philosophers at work, artists destroying themselves against stone and canvas. And here, the grand circle is coming to a close, the big mandala is being accomplished, maybe, even, who knows, the Eternal Return. I'm witnessing, and so are the cleaning woman and the Prime Minister of France, a nation-state's agony, and the merging of all national rivers into the European ocean. Something is dying, at last, so that something can be born. There's little time left to think of Paris in the ways of Napolean III. What will happen to these tiny streets like Rue Férou and Rue Servandoni? Will they become Berlin's cat-alleys, Rome's suburbs, Spain's northern frontier, the center of some platform to Space? All I know is that this thing we loved, or cursed, at times loved with passion, is going under, under before our eyes. This thing, yes, Paris, crucible of all contradictions, window from which you see the whole sky or throw yourself into the street and die, like cats thrown aside in the gutter with a kick from your foot. That's what it is: a place of stability on which one can never rest. Are we condemned to proceed in circles? I love a circularity which brings me back to all that I'm avoiding. This repetition is incarceration, for some. It's also, for others, a relentless initiation to the self. The small theatres where actors imitate their own lives' poverty exude some strange energy that spills over on us. Too many words, too little of anything else; and I don't dare pronounce the word love. Words, in Paris, would fill mountains. Where's the city where no one talks? You would think that it would be a cemetery. It wouldn't. The dead speak more than we do. Isn't that what Paradise is about? So where is that city? Here go the bells of Saint-Sulpice. They speak, too. Round, sonorous, sounds. Calls to the Sunday collection. In the meantime, the sky moved. I saw it. A dome which rotates on its axis. A dome with no ceiling. The midday light pushed the clouds aside, didn't like what it saw, and receded. The clouds are back, noisy children of the sky, tomorrow's rain. There's voyage in the air, Michelangelo waiting. It's time for all colors to stand and mix. Where the trumpets? If only these colors will move and refresh the scene I will give them my love. Here I am, fallen from high into a yellowish excavation under a greyish sky. It doesn't lead to happiness. Paris is a snare. We're no foxes or rabbits: if we were, we would have escaped, or died. We do neither. Our dying is imperceptible. All people in buses are dying organisms. Some have reproduced themselves, some have not, like pigeons, fat and dark, birds of no good tidings. The weather is stormy. Something will burst: if not my patience, the sky. The air will burst. We're moving towards something which does not exist. The voyage is infinite. The passenger is not. The programmer is for keeps. The program has gone astray. The script is perpetually in a foreign language. Don't approach it, it's useless. Sometimes, it's not even THERE.

Why has the sky lifted so high as to let a luminous blue turn it into a flowers' field? Is the city by its sheer power connecting itself with the rest of the universe? Am I part of that effort? Digits have programmed this infinity into which we are sucked, and still, what a company! Stars all over the place, lanes of darkness and fire! This perverse moment turns me into a sponge and beatitude flows through. No, this doesn't mean that I will be fooled into believing that electric waves are angels. The sense of pure space can lead to doubting the existence of anything else, one's self included, and bring about destruction. So I have to take hold of myself and return to Paris's streets with no other parachute than my will. How hard, how stupid, to leave any part of the sky for a terrestrial spot. But is Paris on this planet, or has it been constructed by extraterrestrials in order to be such a mixture of paradise and hell as to confuse the human race and keep it riveted to it? All I know is the here and now, and accumulation of neon lights pushing into oblivion a warm yesterday. In the dark I can read the shop signs which try to catch customers and turn the streets into a dictionary of shop names. Add all the newspapers, the names of libraries, churches, cafés and boulevards, all this unsolicited readings, and you get a jungle of words which is a little hellish. I hear you say no, and I wonder. Come on! you say, Madame de Sévigné's courtyard, hell?

Of course not. I'm not going into that. It's raining again. My bones speak better than my head. They deal with certitudes. They store such knowledge of the weather that I respect them more than I respect myself. We're made of water and bones, strange! Why do we need temples made of marble? Temples, for the past, electrons, for the future. The present time will be overlooked. Let everyone be displeased. It's time for a break at the Café de la Mairie. It won't give much comfort, though. Such a messy place. But it has energy. Little amounts of money circulate constantly, and there's good draft beer, the smell of fries coming out of the kitchen. It's crowded, rather unfriendly. But it's home, in a special way. The garçons are as grumbly as stepmothers. But when a customer trips over a chair, they show good care, shake their heads, enter long conversations. In the summer the terrace is under wonderful shades. In the Café de la Mairie I do my daily thinking. I not only evoke Djuna Barnes, yes, always, and remember her as she was sitting in her New York studio, on Patchin Place, living in the penumbra of her fame, but do also my daily trivial meditations. Right now, I'm looking around me. Men and women of various ages stare at the trees in front of them. I can add their ages, and it amounts to many centuries. I am surrounded by centuries of time spread differently than we're used to think. So I enter a new Time measure, I am contemporary with two thousand years! And what about the languages these people speak? I'm hearing secret thoughts in probably Vietnamese, Arabic, Italian . . . who knows? And now that Russia is going through the most atypical period of its history, I may be sitting next to a neighbor who speaks Ukrainian to himself. It's scary to be in the Café de la Mairie de la Place Saint-Sulpice. Too much of time, too much of space, too much of history, too many words in too many languages. I should run away. But there's something hypnotic in sitting by a table which gets messed up and cleaned at least once every half hour, and in being anonymous in spite of my daily visit, knowing too well that I could disappear without anyone in here ever asking a question. I stand up, button my coat, wear my hand-knitted bonnet, throw a few coins on a little plate, and poorer by some change, richer by some minutes, or, rather, older, slightly but surely, I go out, and to make my way longer, take Rue des Canettes, go into my familiar alleys, and here I am in front of a large door which requires a key. I hesitate. Do I have any key to anything? If I don't know the physical laws that make a car function, how would I know the larger questions. It's easy to answer questions; the hardest part is to find them. My courtyard is so rigidly determined. I'm so much doomed to be unable to affect it in any way, to change its size in any direction, that I had to accept this defeat which determined the previous ones, and the ones to come.

Cities attract each other like flowers do; they form a
secret society and you can't get involved with one of them
without being solicited by the others. Rejection and attrac-
tion are their favorite games. What are the relations between Paris and Aleppo? Here you breathe rejection;
wouldn't you breathe alienation in a Syrian city of the
North? The question has to be answered if the Earth is to
continue to turn. It's raining again. I forgot my raincoat.
I'm walking simultaneously on many tracks: standing on
Aleppo's Citadel I'm also standing by this red light, getting
wet, and I'm walking the streets of Beirut where a snow
storm is raging. My thoughts seem to be going East,
towards Russia. Oh! if only Paris could get blanketed by
snow. I wish it would. But European unity has not yet per-
formed such a miracle. It's too soon to tell. The Neva is
white and broad. At home, I'll read *The Rhine*. Make comparisons with the Seine, I mean I'll let the Seine make
them. You're too wet to be any good, says the Rhine to the
Seine. Let's not start a Franco-German war, replies the
Seine. And that's all for today. Don't people in Paris ever
make a living with solid work? Oh yes they do! They work
a lot, but slowly, because hurrying would show a lack of
manners, and this holds true for the plumber or the sales-
man. And where are the children? They're made invisible
by their blue coats which match their blue stockings. Sad

little things with heart-breaking smiles. Too soon in their lives they're brought to school and sometimes it rains on them through the stairways. Parisian stairways can provoke enduring passion. Full-fledged beings, incorporated into our nervous systems, they can gain on us. I have no need of them, having an elevator. I am heading for the slaughter-house of many an expectation: to the Prefecture, where I will renew my residency. Everything is bothersome about that trip. Just out of the metro I'll face a flower market, a treacherous one, hiding within itself a market for rabbits and hamsters, for birds, some of which are as small as a thumb, all encaged and piled on top of each other. The smells, cries for help, the confusion and desperation of these little beasts make a sinister preparation for the similar emotions and thoughts which overtake, one hundred yards further, the refugees and foreigners who queue for their papers, arriving at dawn. Of course Paris cannot absorb the entire globe in population terms, and the world sees in Paris ultimate salvation. What an incredible misunderstanding! But when my papers will get properly stamped, I, the stranger who at times is more French than the French, will go to the corner Brasserie and instead of ordering a late lunch, will ask for a grand café au lait, taking time off. I may look at the sky, once, or twice; speaking its own perfect French, I'll address the weather: it's good to have one's papers in order, I'll say, not to be obliged to leave, to have a whole year without fearing the police, and before starting to worry about the possibilities of falling ill, and the bills

that will have to be paid, it's good to feel, even if it lasts
only an hour, a long stretch of time following the café au
lait, good to look again at the sky, at the little blue that
appears in it, to feel secure, or to say it truly, *eternal.* Do
women, then, walk more invisibly than men? I don't
know. I can't see myself come down a street, toward some
other form of my own self. I'll therefore settle for incom-
plete certitudes. With all my official papers resting in their
drawers, and being sure that the rain is not pouring, I'll
come out of my flat in the late evening and take the bus to
the Lebanese restaurant Rue Frédéric Sauton. Its proximity
to Notre-Dame relates it to the Middle Ages and in fact it is
medieval food that they serve: mint, onions, olive oil,
sesame, chick peas, minced meat, pine nuts, honey, everything that comes down from medieval Arabia. It's nice to
be close to the River and to the stained-glass windows of
the cathedral, even if they're invisible at night, from that
distance. They are there, protecting our meanderings. You
don't fear hunger, in such places, neither fear poverty of the
spirit. Close, again, to water and stone, near the symbols of
ancient European unity and Arab History, I can dismiss the
present as a passage. The trouble, though, is that I don't
know where I come from, and even less, where I'm heading for.

Dear Parents, why did you lie to me? You told me the
sky was blue while we watched it together, in Beirut, by
the sea, and the sunset was a flame. You fooled a whole
generation, then you destroyed it, the city is destroyed.
The sky is not high, either, as you taught me, it is so low,
low, below my ceiling. I wonder if the rain will come in
and spoil my books as it does my bones. I feel them, tonight, these bones you gave me. Neither one of you ever
saw Paris, or intended to. Your trains never ended at Gare
de Lyon. You thought of France as an intruder into the
order of things as you knew them. Paris was a place of per-
dition, you said. Be reassured: I did not lose my soul in it. I
only lost my illusions. And you. But they used to make
good movies with such experiences. They knew how to
mix fog with love; white sheets, with death; eyelashes,
with long shadows. Paris walks all over my heart, and it is
a city in a constant hurry, I say it often. A city for the ex-
pectancy of love. What a missing ingredient of our imagination love is! It's the unknown particle that makes all
theories fail and lose their minds. Dear Parents, how can I
make sense to you? I will have to leave you for ever. When
I try to walk freely, I am hampered by the army of dogs
that the city keeps in its apartments. The sidewalks are
messed up to an unbearable degree. But can one curb the
citizens' freedom? In this capital of solitude it will take a

Roman emperor of the Late Period to deprive the old folks of their sole companion. Dogs keep Paris sane. Much more than cats. Paris is not Naples: therefore it doesn't worship cats. It's a rational city and dogs are more rational than cats, or monkeys. I didn't say more intelligent. Anyhow, I wouldn't keep an animal. I might be in danger. The danger of mimicry. This is a terrifying possibility, to become a donkey, or a horse, suddenly. What would my neighbor say, she who never saw a cow. Intellectuals in this city pride themselves of having lost some of their senses, like smelling, or hearing. They don't listen to music, they talk, or read, about it. So they won't enjoy the vision of me galloping over their books. They will behave as if they never knew me. Gone, all the friendships. No one is allowed to change species. And those who transgress their gender lose their friends. And what of a woman still in love with a man who became a woman? It's true that Parisians, the most provincial of all city-dwellers, love Sappho. But the poets don't invite her to the café. For one thing, she doesn't write in French, and if she did, being Greek, she would be called *francophone*. I don't mind their boorishness towards Sappho, it's too late for her to care. It's more serious a matter when they ignore the story-tellers of Senegal. Africa is literature made flesh. Oh! an icy wind blew over me. Could it be that it came from Moscow, where so much turmoil comes from? Dear Parents, you never guessed right: you thought Russia was immutable, like the desert, and you stopped speaking French when buying oranges. I'm telling you—now that it is too late—that the countries you knew have disappeared, like your empires. Paris doesn't disappear. It has no intention of being heroic and starting wars it will lose. It has jewelry stores in its belly, all the peacetime trades. Its atomic bombs are tested elsewhere. The radiation is kept in Melanesia and you can't find a map of that archipelago in Paris. You have to go to the Vatican to find one. You know why. In the bookstores you can find all the books proper to print. The improper ones are aborted in early pregnancy. So reading the papers is enough to keep your ignorance going. I sit in the café, where it doesn't matter if it's raining or not, and in *Le Monde* I read so much on human rights that I wonder who are these people who have so many rights? I will not start enumerating those who don't have any, because it may encompass the whole planet. I will do like Commandant Cousteau and plunge undersea and look for sharks in the Red Sea. They're so gentle compared to the people that surround me. I won't mind if one of them wants to eat me. Salt water will help its digestion.

PARIS, WHEN IT'S NAKED

Now that the mist has lifted letting a dying sun send myriads of lit particles into the air, I can walk in this celestial dust with a new freedom. I love the river in this moment, with adolescent passion. It flows so hurriedly. Its color plays on my brain like a live being, a child running there, in these mysterious neurons that determine this moment and this flow. The riverbank is large and empty. I love desperately the walls that limit the current; they're tall, stone built, and I tell myself that they remind me of my particular Orient, old Damascus's stones, and even Rome. Yes. Paris is a nordic city with a mediterranean culture, and that's why it's a maddening place. You can never escape that equation. Where am I? The bridges are made of stone, like the ones which straddle the Tiber. Why, why Damascus haunting Paris, why the Mediterranean under this familiar light? History took its time, here, bringing gradually its ingredients to the peasants of the North. The fire was strong enough to reach the Seine's embankments. Here, it became regal. I sense the hands that built this open canyon through which the city's blood runs to the ocean. Such beauty enslaves more than any conquest. The definition of the soul is made of these places where you feel that the world came into being so that they could exist. That's what we are: beings made through the contact of water with stone, of a chilly sunset with pure geometry. My hands touch the remnants of the day's warmth on cobblestones, walls, moorings. In this moment no boats are going up or downstream. Three elements concur here: the river, the walls, and me. I will sit here. My thinking will reach low fire, my various desires will vanish. Now I am water, and the wall's surface, and then I am a flow, and a line, and further on I become many, or one, of the dimensions of Being, maybe the basic molecule of Time. Here. It's always here. It's only through this ultimate solitude reached by the very fact of living, that one can find the kind of peace that makes tangible the accumulated absurdities that constitute every one's personal truth. Yes. Paris has to be reduced to energy points, has to be obliterated, and then rebuilt by one's mind, to be livable. Otherwise you become car fumes, pornographic junk, a ball of hatred, the most fallen of the banished angels. Back to the street. The buses are full of standing passengers, and beggars crowd the metros. In some police station some stranger is kicked in the stomach and politicians plan their next predatory assault on Cambodia. Good. The human race has no excuse. The Beast has to roam in the forest he made for himself. Look at all the things he needs, the needles, the irons. Why so much clutter? The churches are closed at night so that the homeless remain unsheltered. Cities, who is going to tell what you are? This one, at least, has a few things I know. It is the Niagara Falls of words. There isn't a second, day or night, when millions of people aren't talking. Speech never stops, not counting the stream of words that we carry within. Could we have silent television? It would be a Revolution to surpass 1789. If Paris stopped talking it would be after an atomic war, and even that's not a sure proposition. Let's keep atomic wars away . . . the most talkative city is after all an aviary, so many birds chirp in it. They are all most happy when they talk about their miseries, so no one takes a Parisian seriously. Anyway, the French pretend to dislike seriousness as much as I dislike their pigeons. I appreciate the things they're not responsible for, such as the cloud formations over the countryside. This exaggeration soothes my spirit. We have no fists against the world's ills, I mean the Gulf War and the heroics of Operation Daguet. I was sitting and watching a storm bigger than the Deluge. It's not my heart which broke, no, it's something so enormous that I'm blinded. Fire brings smoke and the thick smoke on the desert reached Paris. The sky disappeared, the earth crumbled under my feet, and my vision dimmed. The pain was slow and steady. Empires are eagles, it must be true. They hover. Archangels don't descend on celestial cities. They're replaced by what we have seen. Does that mean that adding to the injury, I love my enemy? It may be. Should I not belittle love? Maybe I would. An enemy is always within the walls. Intramuros. He's always facing us, traveling along, across the table, sitting in a café. I see him sure of himself, a falcon, a vulture. Then I realize that I'm not his prey. So I turn my back and start the long walk along the sacred way, through hundreds of Greek temples, to the Luxembourg Gardens. Paris opens its gates. They came from everywhere in the world, for centuries, bringing the best they had. It's the keeper of the world. It doesn't belong to itself, it doesn't belong. This is why it's circular. More Spanish than Spain, more Germanic than the Visigoths, more Arabian than Mecca, more Italian than Dante, more of a desert than the desert, it is living in one's mind like the turning center of everything that is.

PARIS, WHEN IT'S NAKED

This morning, as I was walking down Rue des Canettes, the roadway was wet and light was falling from the skies. It was a good feeling. I turned the corner, by the café; the mirror was shining. Such moments renew the world. *Aux Trois Canettes* was not yet open. I threw a glance through its window into its darkness and the magic night of Christmas came back to my memory. It is not too long ago that we spent Christmas eve in this Italian place: I had thought that its owners would be as homesick as I for the Mediterranean, and, in fact, they must have been, given that they were even nicer than usual. At 9 p.m. the restaurant was still without customers. Embarrassing. Were we, Simone and I, behaving like transients? No. We had decided not to let morose ideas invade our minds. Toward our main course's middle, an old man came and sat at a small table. Another one followed, hung up his hat and his coat, sat next to him, but barely acknowledged his presence. Christmas meant watching these two lonesome beings avoid talking to each other. They were each smiling to the *patron,* smiling, yes, for every fork, knife, or napkin that was being set in front of them. We were having a memorable Christmas, all our own. A young couple entered into this subdued atmosphere. We ordered some more wine. Suddenly, lowering her inimitable voice, Simone said: look, they must be deaf, he's speaking to her in sign language. She's so beautiful! Yes, their faces were indeed radiant. Their happiness wasn't making a single sound. We were all having a silent night indeed. I'm walking in the same street and I can't make up my mind about that night. Was I numb, then, or is Paris too cold and damp, these days, for me to cheer up memories? Does memory have its own laws? Is it ours, or not? Something is pursuing me which seems to belong to eternity, I can't reach it, as if my inner eyes were short-sighted. I should hurry. My poet friend is waiting. Yes, I saw him at the Saint-Claude. When we finished talking about writers who write on writing, and those who, having carefully and symbolically murdered their wives, turn their stories into series, we addressed the subject of summer vacations. While I stayed in Paris and had taken fifteen to twenty cups of coffee at the Flore, they didn't bring back the tritest discovery . . . Not that I expected them to bring back a buffalo. But I'm sure that they didn't even notice the size of their spoon on the Greek island. They returned impoverished but confirmed in their own worth. I stayed in my apartment where I will welcome any dream. I'm back in the street, musing, or at home, admiring the fine craftsmanship of the ceiling's moldings, not flying. Oh yes! I'll have to go to Rue Vavin, to the furniture store, and buy a couch. Sitting will be comfortable in the one I saw a few days ago. I'll sink in it, every day a bit lower, and my neighbor will knock at my door wondering why so much noise is pouring out from my windows while I'm known for being a very quiet person. Dear people, let the city follow its course, light its street lamps, measure its shadows, let me look for a blanket, it's a cold night. Time will always be with us.

PARIS, WHEN IT'S NAKED

We are engaged in the search for progression. A story. But some lives do not make a coherent story, all they do is make a sound. In these streets on which no one leaves traces, people are phantasmagoric propositions. Why aren't we expecting something from them, a smile, a nod? We could have been friends. But they're strangers to each other, even those who are French. It makes no difference. This is why great actresses die young in this city: they realize sooner than we do that life is a stage. The play is not written, the actors do not rehearse. They don't know where they stand. They deal with illusions under winter's protection, because the city is the capital of Absence, it's haunted. All those who disappeared in the past live here, so people arrive from all over the world to think about them, to lend them their own imagination's life. Some of them died recently. We lost them. The sense of loss finds its natural habitat in Paris. We measure losses . . . To lose Yourcenar, to lose Delphine, is to lose beings who give rise to the sensuousness of the spirit, to the desire to love. To lose them means the loss of the *self*. Further on, creeks run, large branches from oak trees make a curtain of lace over the water. These creeks are far away. In Northern Italy. When cataclysms will have distorted the world the Italian cities of the North will form an intact kingdom of beauty, this because of Leonardo who saved them by his grace. But when you live here long enough you have to believe, against all odds, in the possibility of salvation. It is in big cities such as this that one can look for personal salvation. Salvation has nothing to do with religious theorems: It is a plant which functions like a cactus: it grows, and hurts, and doesn't need water. It transforms the heart's desert into a night landscape. Thus in the heart we seek refuge. I want to be saved, even if I don't know exactly what it means, and have to solve two essential notions. I will start with the notion of Time. No book has yet clarified for me this thing by which we live and die. But one evening, in San Francisco, at Spec's, Jack Hirschman told to my ear this story: someone asked Yogi Berra: What time is it? and Berra said: You mean, *now*?! We laughed, and while we were laughing, and Jack was drinking beer, and Csaba was thinking about the world's ills, and women and men were shouting, the secret of Time had been broken, in a flash, thanks to

Yogi's moment of distracted perception. Watches can keep working, they don't intrigue any more. Time has changed its nature. So, Paris is a box for toys, each building a child's real-life model, its stores magic chambers where you enter with paper bills and exit with carefully wrapped packages. In the meantime your mind pursues its monologue, you repeat words, thinking they're ideas. Let's be direct: you think of death. And what is death? Disappearance, I should say. A magician's trick: here's the handkerchief, here it isn't! No. It's something else. It's inbuilt in life. But that doesn't say what it is, it being the end of life. Death is not a fact. It's a judgement passed on a fact, accompanied by pain, or, rather, by fear. Fear of what? Fear of death. I sit in my café and keep reflecting, pushing here and there. In Southern Morocco the cactuses have grown. But I'm back in Paris, for sure. The sky is here, luminous with, again, much silver in it, and freshness. Ideas and the weather go hand in hand, each modifying the other. The light is scaled down fractions of a degree, and we sink with it, in the sky's greyness. A cloud moves east, we recognize that it is going away from the sun, and our heart tightens, gives up on a thought that was approaching. We're never who we were. I'll be daring and order some beer on an empty stomach. But what is death? Life is so silly and formal around here that I can't ask my neighbors. What is it? It is the breakdown of unity, of the ultimate unity of the self. This breaking down is death. Death started with Time, not with Life. Life WAS. That moment when death was not yet existing gave birth to Time, which means it gave birth to its own death. So death and time are interchangeable. Death is another name for Time. And that will be my salvation. At least for today.

PARIS, WHEN IT'S NAKED

In fairness to my imagination I should say that the VIème arrondissement was built by Baudelaire. He's still around, following the young poets who inadvertently walk past his birthplace. Baudelaire is in a state of perpetual reincarnation. Do you have an English version of his poems? I ask the lady at the Village Voice. It's a perverse question, I know. Then I tell her that he's not alone in his after-death. He's coupled with Delacroix. For ever. The poet and the painter became Siamese twins, or, rather, I should say that the former drowned in his fateful verse:

Delacroix, lac de sang hanté des mauvais anges.

I spend long hours with him in the Luxembourg, when the gates are closed and the little boats on the octagonal fountain, gone. We stay late into the night on a bench, under the black trees, and can't see the sky and the clouds. Our thoughts keep us warm. Our intimacy with the city makes words superfluous. In a sweet quietude I share with him the sentiment of the self's dissolution and recall *Fusées:*

112

Ivresse religieuse des grandes villes.—Panthéisme.
Moi, c'est tous; tous, c'est moi.

And then slowly I go through national disasters, my heart getting heavier, espousing the cobblestones, my mind descending, literally, going downward, seeking darkness, getting to the earth's central stillness. Sometimes there appears on the horizon a glimmer, a deliverance in the form of a special bookstore which is in my neighborhood, in front of which I walk very often, but on the opposite sidewalk, wishing not to disturb the awesome assembly of writers it contains. It's a shady place, a friendly one, needless to say, on a gentle street named Rue Princesse. On its shelves American writers become the expatriates they always yearned to be. But I don't stand much around books. An ancestral forest within me stirs my memory and makes life untenable. My brain, fearing to explode, directs my steps again to the Church of Saint-Sulpice. In there I find my other forest, a perennial one, where I walk regularly, and which is made of a few square meters; it haunted Baudelaire with its symbols and Delacroix with its depth. With the world deteriorating as it's doing, we shall go more and more to the works which bear witness to its essential grandeur. Jouve named the masterpiece "Jacob and the Angel of the Lord," but who are they, these who make the triad in which we're enclosed? We could say that Jacob is you and me, and that the angel we're fighting is the City, its power on the world, but then, Who, the Lord? It looks to me that the supernatural is nowadays riding in taxis which spit out women ridden by disease who take elevators to rooms where eager men buy their bodies and their souls while female pimps wait in the glistening night for a share of the money. In the morning these night creatures queue in front of hospitals, shrieking with pain when diagnosed sick and obsolete . . . and we move on with our vision blurred by the rain. But how can I give up on this city where every encounter, every talk, becomes a moment of truth? Delacroix confided one day that he had in his heart "something black to satisfy." That blackness is the substance of Paris, the city which makes the will infinite and gives to one's fancy inexhaustible forms. But that makes me wonder why my friend M.F. went so regularly (and secretly) to San Francisco. It's true that San Francisco is a shadow-play, and there, he used to tell me, once the sunset was over, he would take a promenade, dressed as a woman, giving himself to whatever the fog would hold. We are speaking here of a charcoal night descending upon us all, we're gossiping about human miseries, letting the city's sounds penetrate us and become our own thoughts. My friend was much attracted to the agonies of incarceration, and died imprisoned in a sickness. He lived what he had imagined. What happened? I think that he was ruled by the imagination which is everyone's shadow. When the mind reaches the imagination's deepest end, the imagination gives in but remains intact and active. Then our mind, under the pressure of unleashed impulses, shatters all the interdicts we know into bits and pieces. The imagination feeds then on these pieces as flames on fuel.

The mind, left without its shadow, ends up walled in into itself, into its own hell. Death becomes inevitable. I see it waiting around the corner, as if it were a person, pretending to look at windows, entering sometimes a photography store, sometimes a flower-shop. It looks sideways and peers into mirrors. It pretends to love the city and sits in a café, among people, pretending to be absent-minded while listening carefully to conversations. It crosses the street watching the traffic lights. It follows some passerby that it chooses at random and sometimes strikes a conversation with him, or her. I tell it that some people stay young when transplanted, that I am myself, maybe, an old child, moving slowly along the walls of the Préfecture . . . It disappears in the fog with which my body is fused, the rain continues to fall on my face and on my tears, and my spirit behaves like a migratory bird. Then my spirit lands anew, the food is ready, at the time when one half of Paris's population comes home and the other half gets ready for its nightly hunt. My day is not over yet. Darkness smoothes out the edges of my heart.